WESLEY ELLIS

LONE STAR

AND THE
TRAIL TO ABILENE

JOVE BOOKS, NEW YORK

LONE STAR AND THE TRAIL TO ABILENE

A Jove Book / published by arrangement with
the author

PRINTING HISTORY
Jove edition / February 1992

ISBN: 0-515-10791-3

Jove Books are published by The Berkley Publishing Group,
200 Madison Avenue, New York, New York 10016.
The name "JOVE" and the "J" logo
are trademarks belonging to Jove Publications, Inc.

PRINTED IN THE UNITED STATES OF AMERICA

10 9 8 7 6 5 4 3 2 1

LONE STAR

AND THE
TRAIL TO ABILENE

★

Chapter 1

Jessie untied a bandanna from her lovely face and used it to mop her sweaty brow. The dust was so thick that she had to replace the bandanna as she surveyed the big herd of Texas Longhorn cattle that her cowboys had just finished gathering. The cattle were not as sleek and fat as Jessie had hoped, and that was strictly due to the drought that gripped West Texas.

Her immense Circle Star Ranch should have been covered with tall spring grass, affording plenty of forage for the steers, but with almost no water, the range was powder-dry, and watering ponds that were normally full now lay baked and crusted with cracked mud.

Jessie turned to look at her samurai who was mounted on a fine pinto gelding. Ki also wore a bandanna over his mouth and nostrils and even though Jessie could not see his expression, she knew it would be a scowl. Ki was half Caucasian, half Japanese, and a martial arts expert. He could run like a deer, fight like a wildcat, and outlast even the toughest Apache warrior. But he could not even pretend to enjoy acting the part of a cowboy. Ki was far more comfortable afoot than on a horse, and Jessie knew he endured these long spring trail drives north because he was committed to being her best friend and protector.

Jessie was just about to say something to cheer her samurai when Ed Wright, the Circle Star foreman, came galloping up to her side.

"The count is just over seventeen hundred," he said. "The boys are still shaggin' a few more head out of the brush, but we'll go with less than two thousand this year."

"That's still more than we've ever driven to market before," Jessie said.

"I'm afraid we ain't got any choice but to send a few cows along with the steers, Miss Jessie," Ed told her with a sad shake of his head. "The feed is so light this spring, the range is overstocked."

"I know."

Jessie watched as a cowboy bolted after a brindle steer who tried to break from the morning's gather. The cowboy's horse was a big dun, and as it chased after the steer Jessie thought the horse looked sluggish and weary. Hell, she thought, we're all weary. This has been a hard roundup.

"Maybe we shouldn't take any of our cows to market," Ed muttered. "It's a damn waste to take a two- or three-year-old cow and sell her off for butcher beef."

Ed Wright was a cattleman from his boots to the crown of his tall Stetson, and Jessie knew that it pained him greatly to sell off young breeding cows and heifers, the foundation of any good herd.

"We'll raise more," she said. "And we've gone over this already. We both know it will be a lot easier to sell cows than to watch them starve before the rains come this fall."

"*If* they come this fall."

2

Ed glanced up at a cloudless sky, scorched a pale blue by endless weeks of blazing sun. "We may be in for several more years of this. It's happened before."

"Don't remind me," Jessie said. She sighed. "It's been almost twenty years since we've seen the range this dry in April. We need rain worse than I can ever remember."

Ed dismounted wearily. He and the Circle Star cowboys had been rounding up cattle for almost a month now, and it had been hot, dusty, and hard work. Men, horses, and cattle were all worn down to nothing.

Jessie watched her foreman unsling and then uncork his canteen. Ed poured water into the palm of his big, calloused hand and splashed it across his face. There was so much dust on his skin that it turned to mud and ran. Ed drank, offered some of his water to Jessie and Ki, and when it was refused, he removed his battered Stetson, filled it and let his horse drink.

Jessie squinted up at the sun, then back to Ed as he climbed stiffly onto his lathered mount. Ed was in his forties, a tall man, tough as rawhide but unable or unwilling to pace himself during these roundups, so she often had to order him to slow down. Right now, he looked worn to a frazzle. His eyes were sunken from lack of sleep, and the hollows of his cheeks were very deep from too much work and too little rest.

"Ed," Jessie told him, "I want you to finish this roundup by tomorrow."

"But we can't do that! We'll miss at least a couple of hundred that we could drive north."

"We've got enough," Jessie told her foreman. "Those that we leave behind will just have to forage for themselves. Any more time spent here will make driving the herd that much more difficult for all the others. Besides, we'll be striking out across new territory. If we follow the other herds, there wouldn't be enough grass to feed a flock of gophers, let alone these hungry cattle."

Ed glanced at the samurai. "You better bring all your weapons, Ki. We'll be going across Comanche land and they'll want this herd now that most of the buffalo are

3

killed off by the damned hiders."

"We'll do what we have to do," Ki said matter-of-factly.

"I'll give them a few dozen of my cattle," Jessie said, "for the privilege of passing across their lands."

"They might want the entire herd," Ed told her. "The buffalo hunters have taken away their livelihood and they're bitter as hell."

"They have a right to be." Jessie said, her expression grim, "but I can't allow them to take my cattle."

Jessie and Ki exchanged glances. After being around each other for several years and having more than their share of harrowing adventures, they could almost read each other's minds.

"We're up against a rock wall," Jessie said. "We can't feed the cattle here and we can't go north up the main trails. That only leaves us the choice of going across Comanche lands."

"We'll make it," Ki said.

"You hope," Ed grunted out loud. "But I do know this much—every cowboy on the Circle Star payroll is plenty ready and willing to do whatever it takes to get this herd to market."

"I know that," Jessie said, "and it makes me proud to hear that the men are behind me all the way. So tell them to finish things up and let's start north in three days. That will give us a little time to rest up and get our wagons and provisions in order."

"Yes, ma'am," Ed grunted, reining his horse around and starting to ride away.

"Ed?"

The foreman turned back to Jessie. "Yes ma'am?"

"I want you to slow down a little. Don't be so hard on yourself, the cowboys, and the livestock. We've got a long, hard trip ahead."

"I know that, Miss Jessie. But every steer we can trail north is one less that I'll be worrying about this summer. I got a hunch that, as we move north, there might be some pretty good grass for these cattle. Used to be the

4

finest buffalo graze in the country. Sometimes we get a little better rains up north in the Panhandle Country."

"I hope you're right about that," Jessie said. "And I hope that we can make a truce with the Comanche."

"So do I," the foreman said. Then he patted the gun at his side. "But just in case we have to fight, we'd better arm every man with an extra gun and cartridge belt. Better make sure they ride with Winchesters, too."

"They won't be happy with rifles slapping underneath their knees for that long a ride," Ki said.

Jessie agreed. A rifle could be a real nuisance in brush country, snagging up a man and horse and even creating a hazard. "We can keep the rifles in the wagon and bring them out only if we sense an attack."

"You can 'sense' one?" Ed asked suspiciously. "I never figured a white man or woman could read an Indian's mind."

Ki shifted in his saddle. "Men who are ready to fight usually exhibit certain signs no matter what their race or culture."

Ed opened his mouth to say something, then closed it and spurred off toward the gathered herd. Jessie watched him signal a few cowboys to come with him and then they rode north up a steep canyon and disappeared in the dust.

"He should have changed to a fresh horse before going out again," Jessie said.

"He'll be all right," Ki said. "He knows every foot of this ranch like the palm of his hand."

Jessie nodded with a frown. She rode off toward the remuda where she would trade the bay she now rode for her favorite horse, a palomino named Sun. Sun would finish out the rest of the day, and tomorrow she would return to her ranch headquarters to supervise the loading of the wagons and all the other preparations needed before they started up the long trail north.

The following afternoon, Jessie was at her desk writing memos to be sent to her many operations worldwide.

5

Her father, Alex Starbuck, had started out with a small import shop in San Francisco and built himself an empire that included the ownership of railroads, shipping lines, rubber plantations, and even diamond mines in Africa. Alex had become one of the richest men in the world and had been the target of a diabolical cartel intent on creating a single world economy under its own control. Refusing to knuckle under to the cartel, Alex had been murdered on this very ranch. Only a few years earlier, she had lost her mother to this same evil cartel.

As Jessie finished a memorandum to a steel mill in Pennsylvania that was having some financial difficulties, her Mexican housemaid, Rosita, came softly into her study.

"Señorita," she said with almost no accent, "won't you please come and eat? You need food and rest. It will be a hard trail drive this year and you must be strong."

Jessie laid down her pen and brushed her fingers wearily across her green eyes. She had long, strawberry-blonde hair and a body made to love a man. But now, after a month of gathering cattle in the heat and the dust, her body was simply weary.

"You are right, of course," she said to the Mexican woman, "but there is much yet to be done."

"Let someone else do it," Rosita said.

Jessie managed a tolerant smile. "There are some things that only I can do, señora. But I promise I will come to eat soon."

"And then go to sleep until morning?" Rosita asked pointedly.

Jessie looked up at her housemaid and dear friend. Rosita had been in charge of the house as long as she could remember. She was a tall woman, thick now in the waist, and with large, pendulous breasts. But she was still quite lovely, and Jessie could see the blood of Apache in her features.

"I promise."

Rosita went away satisfied because Jessie was not a woman to break even small promises. Jessie turned back

6

to her paperwork. In truth, she knew that she should have remained at headquarters each year instead of joining the men to drive her longhorn cattle north. But also in truth, she loved the roundup and the trail drives. At the end of each she often swore—never again. But the next spring she found she could hardly wait to get back into the saddle and work the cattle.

Jessie was starting to draft another memo when she suddenly heard the pounding of hooves and a shout from out in the ranch yard. Hearing her name being called over and over, Jessie came to her feet and rushed outside to see one of her cowboys, Bob Hanes, leap from his horse.

"What's wrong!"

"Ed had a bad spill up in Echo Canyon," Hanes said. "He was chasing a steer and his horse stepped in a hole and somersaulted. It landed square on him."

Jessie's hand flew to her mouth. "How bad is he?"

"Busted ribs. Spitting blood and in a lot of pain. Ki and some of the others are bringing him in on the wagon."

"Go to town and get a doctor," Jessie said quickly. She turned to see old Jim Lawson hobble out from her barn. "Jim, we need a fresh horse! Hurry!"

Jim had also suffered a bad fall that had left him partially crippled. But the tone and urgency in Jessie's voice sent him hobbling back toward the corral.

Jessie turned back to Bob. "Bring the doctor straight here. If he's out on a call, find him."

"Yes, ma'am," Bob said, heading for the barn.

Jessie wanted to also get her horse and race off to comfort Ed, but she knew that she needed to prepare for his arrival. Rushing back into her house, she went to a well-stocked medicine cabinet where she kept bandages, splints, and several bottles of medicine, including the strong painkiller, laudanum.

"Señorita, what is it?"

Jessie turned to Rosita. "Ed's horse fell on him. He's pretty badly hurt."

7

"I will prepare a room," she said without any wasted words.

essie was standing on her veranda when the wagon careened into her ranch yard. She had Ki and her men bring Ed into the house, and when he was resting as easy as could be expected, she said, "I've got some laudanum."

But Ed shook his head. Dried blood was crusted on his lips and mustache but there was none in his ears or any other sign of head injury.

"I'll be fine," he breathed.

"You pushed too hard again this year," Jessie told him. "You always do."

Ed's almost bloodless lips formed a thin smile. "I'm going to be just fine in a couple of days and then we can all head out north. This will give the boys a few more days to gather."

Jessie drew a chair up beside her foreman. She looked at Ki and then back to Ed. "I'm going to be needing you to stay here and try to keep things together here."

Protest flared in Ed's eyes. "But . . ."

"Listen to me," Jessie interrupted. "I understand how much you want to help us drive the herd north, but you're needed more right here. You're the only one besides myself who can keep what cattle remaining on Circle Star alive. You know every water hole and blade of grass on this range."

"But you might need me if the Comanche attack!"

"We'll make it," Jessie told him. "And if worse comes to worse, I can lose the trail herd, but I can't afford to lose our foundation herd of breeders. You know that as well as I do."

"Damn!" Ed choked.

"The doctor is coming." Jessie managed a smile. "He's going to make you stay in bed for at least a week. And I want you to eat and fatten up a little, then get ready to take care of things while we're gone. Will you do that?"

Their eyes locked and finally Ed nodded. "You know I'll always do whatever I can."

"Yeah." Jessie patted his arm. "Ed, there's not a finer cattleman in Texas than you. I've often wondered why you didn't start a ranch of your own. I'd have helped."

"I know that," he said. "But when your father hired me years ago, he told me that I would be treated as part of his family and as his friend. And he kept his word. So why should I go off and have all the headaches of ownin' my own spread when I can honcho the finest ranch in Southwest Texas and not worry about it going broke?"

"I don't know," Jessie said. "I never thought of it that way."

"Of course you didn't," Ed told her. "And don't you worry about things here while you drive that big herd up to Kansas. You just stay close to the samurai and be careful."

Jessie nodded. "We'll make it, Ed. We'll be back by fall with a satchel full of money and maybe by then we'll have some good rain and tall grass."

"Yeah," Ed whispered, closing his eyes. "I'm going to go to sleep and dream about that. I surely am."

Jessie left her foreman and went outside to wait for the doctor. She had taken Ed's pulse and his color was good so she was certain that there was no serious internal bleeding.

"He's going to be fine in a week or two," she told her samurai.

Ki nodded and thought of his weapons and of the fierce Comanche warriors whose lands they would have to cross to the north.

★
Chapter 2

The sun was still buried in the low, dark hills to the east when Jessie, Ki, and twenty of the Circle Star Ranch's best cowboys rolled out of the bedrolls, pulled on their boots and moved in silence to the huge coffeepot that hung simmering over their campfire.

Jessie said little because these were almost all veteran cowboys who needed few instructions. Their cook, Scotty Duggan, was a crusty old man in his early sixties who had been on one of the first Texas trail drives when the best market for longhorns was in New Orleans. Scotty, like so many cowboys, had finally gotten too old and rheumatic to take the pounding of a saddle horse. Rather than take up rocking a chair in Houston, Fort Worth, or San Antonio, Scotty had migrated to Circle Star Ranch and talked his way into being an assistant cook. Within two months he'd driven a real cook away with his cantankerous nature and himself become a fair grease and skillet man.

Jessie pursed her lips over her coffee. "We'll want to take it easy for the first few days until the herd builds up to a point where we can cover twenty miles between sunup and sundown."

One of the few cowboys who was not a veteran, Sonny Lane, cleared his throat. "Miss Starbuck?"

"Yes?"

"I understand we're all to be issued rifles."

"That's right."

"We got to carry them on horseback every day?"

"No," Jessie said, speaking to all of them. "Only if you leave sight of the herd to look for the best grass or water up ahead."

Even though his handsome young face was still lax with sleep, Sonny grinned. "Thank you ma'am."

"But," Jessie said, "I want every man to keep an extra cartridge belt in his saddlebags. I don't have to tell you that we'll be breaking in a new trail. The country we'll enter will be hostile. None of us know exactly when or where we'll find water and grass. We're taking big chances but I know that, win or lose, we'll all do our best."

The cowboys nodded. Jessie took a swallow of coffee and shuddered. Scotty's coffee was strong enough to float horseshoes. "Any other questions?"

"How far north do we go before we turn east?"

"Depends." Jessie toed the hard earth. "My thinking and that of Ed Wright was to drive this herd due north at least as far as the Canadian River."

This piece of news brought a few raised eyebrows but no comments. Later, the men would talk, but not now.

"One last thing," Jessie said. "Ki is going to be our eyes and ears. He'll often be out in advance of the herd, sometimes for days. What I want clearly understood is that no one is to pull their gun and open fire. Not at Ki, and not at any Comanche."

"Ma'am?" a cowboy asked, not sure that he'd heard correctly.

"No gunfire unless you are attacked," Jessie said. "Keep in mind that we are going across Indian lands. *Their* lands. I expect to pay the Comanche a fair price."

"What about the Comancheros?" a cowboy named Len asked. "I hear they're thicker'n fleas on a dead dog. They've got a hard reputation and might be even more of a threat to us and the herd than the Indians."

"I've heard the same," Jessie said. "And I'll pay them not one beef or one dollar. The Comanchero are thieves and murderers. They're men without conscience and damn little if any humanity. I'd as soon strike a deal with the devil."

The cowboys had a quick breakfast of beef, bisquits, and gravy, then finished their coffee in silence as the sun began to peek over the eastern horizon. As soon as Jessie washed her own plate, fork, and tin cup, the cowboys followed her example and grabbed their saddles, blankets, and bridles.

"Let's move them out," Jessie said when she was mounted and the sun was edging over the hills, already gleaming fierce and red.

The longhorns were accustomed to being driven and the herd which tallied 1,943 moved north without any fuss. The most aggressive leaders surged to the front of the herd and used their long, sharp horns as they jostled for supremacy. All the cowboys watched to see which of several big steers would assume the overall command.

"There's been some betting on it," a cowboy named Pete Willis said as he rode beside Jessie.

"Who'd you bet on?"

"That big dun steer."

"I think the brindle will come out on top," Jessie said, "or maybe that black and white steer with the blue eyes."

"He's tough," Pete admitted, watching as those three sparred for the lead position until a huge old brindle bull named Horatio with a span of horns at least ten feet wide, and only one eye, bellowed and pushed by all of them to take the lead.

"Well I'll be," Pete said, shaking his head. "Nobody bet on old Horatio taking over again this year. He looks so skinny that he'd go over in a high Texas wind."

Jessie had to smile. It was her policy not to sell her lead bull but instead, to trail him back home to Circle Star after a northern trail drive. In that way, the "boss" of a herd could be expected to set an example the following spring. Rarely if ever, though, did a steer or bull lead the herd up the northern trail two years in a row. It was just too hard, and a younger, stronger animal usually took his turn.

Apparently, however, Horatio had other ideas. And even as Jessie watched, the brindle bull gored its most aggressive companion in the shoulder and fought his way ten yards into the forefront.

"If he can keep up the pace once we get to really moving," Jessie said, "he'll win his life."

"I don't think he can," Pete said. "Last year took a lot out of him and he isn't moving as smooth as he was before."

"Maybe not," Jessie said, "but he's smart and he knows how to pace himself. Perhaps he even remembers that, of the eight steers we started driving back to Texas, he was the only one that we didn't eat on the trail."

Pete chuckled and rode on. Jessie spurred her palomino over to ride alongside of the samurai. Never a talkative man, Ki acknowledged her company with little more than the nod of his head.

"So," Jessie said, "it begins again."

"Yes."

"And what do you see in store for us?" Jessie asked, because Ki had an often uncanny knack for looking into the future.

"I'm not sure you want to know."

Jessie's smile evaporated. "You're wrong. I very much want to know what you think is going to happen."

"I see death and a great deal of trouble in store."

"From Indians?"

The samurai shrugged his broad shoulders. Ki was a slender man, but wiry and far stronger than he first appeared. His body, trained from adolescence to be supple and quick, could do amazing things, and the power of his foot and hand strikes could level or even kill far heavier men.

"Will we get this herd through to the Kansas railheads?"

"Yes."

"But some of us will die?"

Ki nodded.

Jessie tore her eyes from his handsome face and looked ahead. "I don't fear death and I know you don't either," she said. "But some of the cowboys . . . well, I rather lose the entire herd than to lose a single man."

Ki was silent for several minutes and then he said, "It is our karma to struggle. Without struggle, there is no sap in the tree of life. If there is nothing worth struggle and death, then we have nothing."

Jessie allowed herself a half smile. "Is that the great wisdom of some Oriental philosopher?"

"No," Ki said, "it is simply the truth. All who think understand this."

Ki waited a moment and then he added, "This was first taught to me by Hirata. Almost from the day he saved my life."

"You think often of him, don't you."

It wasn't a question because Jessie knew that the old Japanese *ronin,* a word meaning "wave man," had exerted a most powerful influence on Ki.

"I was a starving halfbreed boy. After my American father died and left my mother a widow, she was treated worse than a dog by her own people. You see, the Japanese believe that they are a superior race and that foreigners are lesser than themselves. It was my mother's unforgivable sin that she fell in love with an American sailor."

"Love is not supposed to be wise."

14

"In my mother's case," Ki said, "it was a tragedy. Born of a royal family, she was never forgiven. If she could have gotten to America . . ."

"It might not have been any better here," Jessie said. "You know how often you are taken for being a Chinese and how foolishly and unkindly you are treated."

"Yes," Ki said. "Hirata told me about these things. He taught me to know that men are often cruel and that only by following 'kakuto bugei,' the true samurai's ways, could I be strong."

"And yet," Jessie ventured, "Hirata himself was abandoned by his own people."

"Once a samurai's master dies, he is without purpose. That is why he is called *ronin*—wave man. Someone who has nothing, whose life, like the waves on a storm-tossed sea, are blown about aimlessly. A *ronin* has nothing, is nothing."

"I don't agree with that," Jessie said. "But we've argued about it before and there is no sense in stirring it up again. To me, one person's value should never be based on the life of another. And if something should happen to me, I want you to live life to its fullest."

"I intend to keep you alive to be very, very old," Ki said. "So this talk is meaningless."

Jessie laughed softly. "Very well. I cannot say that I find that prospect unappealing."

Jessie fell into silence as she watched the brindle bull lead the herd over a low, sun-blasted hill. "Right now I am content, not to worry about living a long life, but about whether or not we'll find water today. In this heat, the cattle and horses would only last a few days."

"I will go ahead," Ki said. "I can find water."

"Be very careful."

"I am *ninja.*"

"You are also human," Jessie reminded the samurai.

Ki rode on ahead and kept his pinto horse at a steady lope until he vanished into the shimmering heat waves. Jessie watched him until he disappeared, and she knew that every cowboy on her crew did the same.

15

The samurai really was their eyes and ears and he would sense danger before any of them, and his warning could prove the difference between life and death, success and failure.

"Be careful," she whispered to the heat, the dust, and the wind, "because you are my best, my most trusted friend."

★

Chapter 3

When Ki left the trail drive and rode out ahead, he never looked back. Ahead of him were a long succession of brown, rolling hills. There were few trees and nothing but withered grass. In the low places the land was pocked with old buffalo wallows, and as the miles passed, Ki saw the sun-bleached bones of the once plentiful buffalo herds.

It was difficult for the samurai to imagine that this was spring and that there had once been thousands of buffalo grazing, rutting, and multiplying in this harsh country. The buffalo had been the life's blood of the Comanche, and when they were gone, the Indians had fallen on bitter times. Now, like their brother the Kiowa, the Comanche were faced with a bleak choice—they could either fight to the death, or allow themselves to be driven to the reservations.

Ki admired the American Indian. To the samurai's

17

way of thinking, these native people of the West were tragic, but very brave and noble. Like the samurai, their men lived by the warrior's code and sought an honorable death.

Ki rode steadily all that first afternoon. By early evening, he was completely absorbed in the quest to find good water for the Circle Star crew and their thirsty livestock. Even if he found it over the next hill, Jessie would still have to drive her longhorns far into the night.

But even as he was thinking this, Ki saw a buzzard circling up ahead and thought that it might be a good sign. Often, in a drought-stricken country, death came by a water hole as men or animals waited for their prey.

Ki dismounted and led his pinto up toward a low rise of land. A dozen yards from the summit, he left his horse and crept up to take a view of the country just ahead. The good news was that he saw a valley of grass and water, probably nourished by some underground spring. The bad news was that there were Comancheros camped under some towering cottonwood trees.

Ki flattened against the earth. He counted six white men grouped under the shade of trees. And although Ki was too distant to hear their voices, he could see them gesturing toward a young man and woman who were bound to a tree by heavy ropes.

The hostages were either Mexican or Indian, Ki could not be certain. However, one thing was obvious—they had been through hell. Both of them sagged against the ropes and it was quite some time before the samurai was even sure that they were still alive. Finally, the woman raised her head and then her companion did the same. Ki could not be certain, but he could almost sense that the woman was begging for food, or water.

A moment later, Ki's hunch proved to be correct because one of the Comancheros slowly came to his feet and took a canteen to the woman. He grabbed her long black hair, jerked her head back against the trunk of the tree, and forced water down her gullet.

Ki could see the woman choke as the Comancheros

18

laughed. The man hostage raised his head and spat at the Comancheros. Instantly, the one with the canteen drove his boot up between the hostage's legs causing him to scream.

Ki did not wince at the terrible pain he saw inflicted, but when the Comanchero again drove his boot up between the hostage's legs, he shuddered. The hostage seemed to go insane with his agony and that only caused the big Comanchero to kick him all the more.

The samurai's hands knuckled until they were white with anger, but he lay helpless to do anything but witness the brutal punishment.

Both hostages began to scream. The woman in anger, the man in agony. Two more Comancheros came to their feet and began to torment the pair. One of them ripped the woman's head back and then tore the top of her dress down to her waist, exposing her breasts. This caused another Comanchero to draw his knife and place it at the woman's breast as if he were going to slice it away.

The woman spat in the man's face. Ki saw blood stream down her ribs and although her breast was not cut away, the samurai knew that she had been cruelly sliced. Even so, the woman continued to rail at her tormentors and Ki heard her Spanish curses echoed across the hills.

Ki tensed as the big leader of the Comancheros also drew his knife. There was nothing the samurai could do to save the courageous young man and woman, although he wanted to try.

The Comanchero leader turned on the young Mexican hostage and even as the woman's scream grew shrill and she watched, the Comanchero slit the Mexican's throat from ear to ear.

Ki's guts knotted in helpless fury. He saw blood cascade down the Mexican's chest and saw his body twitch in death. He heard the laughter of the Comancheros echo across the barren hills and drown out the shrieks of the woman.

Moments later, the Comancheros, their blood lust

satisfied, cut the Mexican woman down, tore off the rest of her clothes, and used her at the feet of her gory companion.

"I will kill them all," the samurai vowed bitterly. "Those animals will not live to see another sunrise."

The samurai did not choose to watch all the Comancheros brutally rape the Mexican girl until she lost consciousness. Ki moved back down the hill to his pinto and began to prepare his weapons. He wanted the sun to go down quickly so that he could exact his revenge. His mind, cold and hard, focused on the deadly weapons of the samurai.

His bow and quiver of arrows were oddities in the West. Especially the bow which was light colored with layers of hardwood glued together and then wrapped with red, silken thread. Unlike the bows of the Indian, Ki's bow was oddly shaped and its tips were sharpened so that they could be used as a lance, and the bowstring was rough enough to saw through muscle and tendon.

Ki tested his bow which, when fired, would turn completely around to face him. His arrows were also unusual but as deadly as any seen on the frontier. One of Ki's favorites was called "death's song" because of a ceramic bulb located just behind its point. The bulb had a tiny hole in its center and, as death's song flew, the wind whistled through the hole and caused an eerie, unnerving sound. In many of Ki's most desperate battles, death's song had broken the nerve of his enemies and given him victory instead of defeat.

Ki also examined with great care the arrow the samurai called "chewer" whose head was formed in the shape of a corkscrew. To be impaled in the belly by chewer was to die a thousand horrible times.

"This one is for the big man," Ki said, holding chewer up to the sunset as he visualized again the terrible savagery he'd just witnessed down in the valley far below.

When Ki was satisfied that his bow and arrows were in perfect order, he removed his western clothing and retrieved his *ninja* costume from his saddlebags. This garment was solid black and incorporated a hood which covered his head and face except for his eyes. Loose fitting, it came with a pair of black sandals. It had taken Ki many years of study and hard discipline to earn the right to call himself *ninja*, "the invisible assassin."

The *ninja* were the most feared warriors in all of Japan. They had been trained to endure great hardships and the art of stealth. A *ninja*, in his black outfit, could go undetected where even the stealthy Apache could not go. He was trained to stay in the shadows of the day and to move along the darkest places at night so that he could position himself for a kill. *Ninja* could move past a hundred palace guards and strike without sound. If a *ninja* ever failed his mission, he was to take his own life rather than escape.

The sun was going down as Ki counted the deadly *shuriken* star blades that he kept secreted in his *ninja* costume. The star blades were Ki's favorite weapon. He could draw and throw them with such speed and deadly accuracy that he was a match for even the most deadly of professional gunfighters.

And finally, when the samurai believed himself to be fully prepared to avenge the poor captive Mexicans, he dropped to his knees and lapsed into his own Eastern prayers and meditations. Ki did not call upon a deity to save his life and help him accomplish his deadly mission, but he did ask for power and courage, and for wisdom and the full use of the physical skills that he had spent so many years perfecting.

And at last, when the sun smothered itself into the western hills, the samurai came to his feet and stood before his horse which had been trained to stay ground-tied until it was allowed to move.

"Go," Ki said, removing his reins from the bit and thus letting the horse know that it was free to return to the Circle Star remuda. "Let your hoofprints lead Jessie to this place."

The pinto threw its head in the air. It wanted to go over the hill and down to the Comanchero camp because it

21

could smell the water and the grass. But the samurai did not allow that and so the pinto was driven back toward the cattle drive where its own strong herding instincts would carry it to the Circle Star remuda.

Ki studied the half-wedge of moon that allowed a man to see for a good hundred yards. Ki knew that the Comancheros would be seated around their campfire probably roasting meat on sticks, perhaps even drinking whiskey. Yes, Ki thought, if they are drinking whiskey, I have a good chance of killing them all.

He slipped over the low hills and moved down a little gulley until he came to the valley floor and then he flattened to his belly.

Now he could hear the men talking, see them seated on logs around the campfire. The girl was missing, however, and that did pose a problem. Had they raped her to death and then thrown her body aside?

Ki doubted that very much. The man whose throat had been slit still hung by his bonds. Ki studied the group and also noted that two of the Comancheros were missing, one of them their big leader.

Damnation! Had they taken the girl away? And if so, for what reason? The only logical answer was that they had taken the girl away to trade. But with whom?

Too many questions, the samurai thought to himself as he began to slither through the grass. The horses, Ki knew, would sense him long before the Comancheros. They might well shy or try to run at the sight of a man slipping on his belly through the grass.

Ki angled a wide circle around the horses and it took him nearly two hours to reach the cottonwoods. Once there, however, he unstrapped his bow and reached back over his shoulder for "death's song." This was the arrow that would drive terror into all but the bravest hearts.

Ki nocked the arrow and slipped forward, going from tree to tree. He moved with the silence of a ghost and the concentration of a stalking lion. It was a disappointment that the big Comanchero who had repeatedly booted the poor Mexican and then had slit his throat was missing.

Never mind, Ki thought. I will find that man and if he and another have taken the girl away, I will find them all, and soon. But first, these four men will die.

So silently and with such care did the samurai approach the campsite that he could see beads of sweat on the Comancheros' faces before he drew back his bowstring and held it for an instant before letting it free. Death's song leapt from his hand and it screamed a path through the trees sending the Comancheros to their feet.

"What the . . ."

The man who was about to reach for his gun seemed to rise up on his toes and then stiffen as death's song shrieked a path to his body that ended as abruptly as it had began. The Comanchero clutched the arrow's shaft and then pitched over onto his face.

The next Comanchero did manage to unholster but he could not fire it as chewer corkscrewed into his prominent belly. The man grabbed his gut and howled like a coyote at the moon.

Ki dropped his bow and reached for a *shuriken* star blade. There were two Comancheros left and he had to give them credit for not turning and racing away into the forest. They had their guns in their fists and they saw the samurai at last.

Ki jumped behind a tree as bullets ripped through the darkness to bury themselves into bark. Ki waited patiently until the firing abated, then he stepped into plain view with his arm already cocked over his right shoulder. With a swift forward motion of his arm and a snap of his wrist, he launched a *shuriken* star blade. Its polished steel glittered wickedly in the firelight and then was seen no more as it vanished into the soft flesh of a Comanchero's throat.

"Ahhggg!" the man choked, dropping his gun and grabbing futilely at his severed windpipe.

The last Comanchero went crazy with fear. He emptied his gun, threw it away, and ran like a whipped dog. The samurai went after him. Ki was fast and the Comanchero slow. It was no match. Ki tackled his last enemy, rolled him over, and as the man reached for a knife, Ki drove the palm of his hand into the Comanchero's nose, driving slivers of bone into his brain.

The Comanchero quivered and then his body went limp.

Ki felt no remorse. He came to his feet and went back to each of his victims. Only one man still breathed.

"Where did the other two go?" Ki demanded, kneeling beside the dying Comanchero.

"Go . . . go to hell!" the man screamed, trying to reach for his gun that had fallen nearby.

Ki pushed the gun away. "Did they kill the girl?"

The heavyset man clutched at his leaking belly as if he might be able to hold his guts inside. Ki thought the man too near death to think clearly. But he was wrong.

"The girl will wish she was dead by midnight," the Comanchero hissed through clenched teeth.

"What do you mean?"

The man gazed up at the hooded samurai. "What . . . what are you?"

"I am the man who took your life. I am *ninja!*"

"You . . . you . . . uggghh!"

The fat man's double chins began to jerk up and down and then his whole body bucked in the throes of death as his heels raked dead leaves. Ki stood up and turned away from the last Comanchero with contempt. He moved to the stream and washed his hands and then he removed his hood and washed his face.

What to do now? he asked himself. It would still be several hours before the Circle Star herd arrived. By then, it would be nearly midnight.

And what of the poor Mexican girl? If something terrible were to happen to her by midnight, did not that mean that other dangers were very near?

Ki thought that this was the only explanation so he went to the Comanchero horses. They were spooky and did not want him to come close. He knew they were not only skittish about his costume, but that they could also smell blood and death.

"I will not harm you," he crooned in a soothing voice to a particularly fine black gelding with a white blaze on its face. "I will not harm you."

The tall, black horse snorted nervously but since it was picketed, Ki had no difficulty getting it to accept his touch. Very soon, he had the animal saddled and bridled. Once mounted, Ki circled the camp until he found the tracks of horses leading to the north. Three horses ridden by two Comancheros and one battered, half-dead Mexican girl.

Ki wished he could wait for Jessie and the Circle Star herd. But there was no time. Midnight was only a few hours away. The samurai was certain that this long night of death was far from over. He also had a hunch that the Comancheros were paying a visit to the Comanche or perhaps even the Kiowa. They would pay a good price for a beautiful Mexican girl, even one who had been raped and beaten.

The samurai looked back at the Comanchero camp which Jessie and her cowboys would find before this long night was over. She would, of course, read the signs and learn the story. She would even guess that he had gone after other men, and Ki was sure that she would follow his tracks to wherever they led.

"Let's go," Ki said quietly to the black gelding. "Let's see if this trail leads to even more troubles."

★

Chapter 4

Ki could tell by the way the hoofprints were deeply cupped across long stretches that the Comancheros with their captive Mexican woman were in a hurry. Fortunately, the black gelding Ki rode was strong, fast, and willing. The horse had an easy gallop and seemed tireless as Ki pushed hard across the open country hoping to overtake his quarry before dawn.

But when the stars died and he still had not overtaken the Comancheros, Ki slowed his mount to conserve its strength. The trail had swung to the west and that was good, because as the sun lifted, it was to his back and it did not impair his vision.

This turned out to be extremely important because, one hour after sunrise, Ki approached a narrow, seemingly boxed canyon and saw an Indian guard peering in his direction, trying to shield his eyes from the sun.

Ki jerked his horse around and moved back to a low

ridge where he dismounted and tied his horse. He moved back to the ridge and surveyed the mouth of the canyon for several long minutes. There was no way he could enter the mouth of that canyon without being seen by the guard. Not even *ninja* could be completely invisible and since there was no cover, the Indian would see him and spread the warning.

Ki walked back down to his horse and remounted. If he could not enter the canyon from the front, he would ride several miles around and attempt to enter it from the rear.

Ki was impatient but not careless as he rode the gelding out again and made his wide arc around the canyon and the little set of mountains just ahead. It was almost noon before he was up in the pines and he could smell smoke and cooking meat which told him that the rear of the box canyon was only a few hundred yards ahead.

The samurai again inventoried his weapons. He had retracted his bloody *shuriken* star blades and "chewer," but "death's song" had been too deeply imbedded in flesh and bone and its ceramic bulb had obviously shattered.

When Ki was satisfied that he was fully prepared to meet his enemies, he again slipped on his *ninja* hood and moved through the trees, mindful that other Indian guards might be watching from this higher plateau.

He saw only a fine buck that seemed very unafraid of him as he passed, and when Ki arrived at the rim of the canyon, he was greeted with quite a surprise because the canyon was a Comanche stronghold. There were no less than fifty warriors and many horses, as well as longhorn cattle. Ki had heard of these isolated Comanche strongholds and now, as he bellied down to observe the camp, he could see that this canyon afforded a perfect hiding place.

The canyon's walls weren't that tall, but they were steep and would be very difficult to climb. The floor of the canyon comprised perhaps two hundred acres and it was matted with grass and fed by a nice spring. The Indians had dammed up the spring and even as Ki watched, he saw several old women and more than few children fill adobe jugs and pots.

Ki's attention soon became fixed on a large and very dirty tent that appeared to be the center of activity. He kept seeing warriors moving in and out of the tent. Later, he recognized one of the Comancheros whose tracks he'd followed. It was then that Ki knew that the big leader of the Comancheros and the Mexican girl were inside.

The afternoon dragged by very slowly without incident. Ki suspected that the Comancheros were doing some tough bargaining for the Mexican girl. This suspicion was proven out near dusk when the big Comanchero exited the tent and, a few minutes later, the Mexican girl, still naked and visibly staggering, was shoved outside by a craggy-faced warrior chief.

There was no fight left in the Mexican when the chief called an old woman to wash, then feed and properly cloth her. The Mexican girl just hung her head and walked away as docile as a pup.

Ki frowned. He supposed that he should not have expected the Mexican girl to protest. After all, she'd lost her friend who was probably her husband or perhaps a brother. She'd been raped by all the Comancheros, beaten, and degraded to the point of stupification. The wonder was that she was still on her feet.

The eyes of the warriors below were all on the girl as she was led down to the spring, then made to undress before the entire encampment and wash herself. The distance was great, but Ki could see that the Mexican girl was built very slender but with large breasts and strong legs.

Ki closed his eyes for a few minutes to better think. What was to be done here? He had sworn to kill the Comancheros but his first duty was to save the young woman if it was humanly possible. After she was out of danger, he could settle with the two surviving Comancheros. It wasn't going to be easy, but he had to try.

As darkness fell, the samurai began to search for a path down the steep canyon's walls. He found the best one available and began the hazardous descent, hanging onto little bushes and anything else he could grip. Once, still a good fifty feet above the canyon floor, a bush tore loose in Ki's fist.

Somehow, he managed to hang on and even though several dozen pebbles rolled down the steep wall, they made almost no sound because they were cushioned by grass. Dangling precariously over the earth below, Ki took a long, deep breath and then swung out and grabbed another bush while his toes dug for a crack in the rock. Steadying himself, he continued to inch his way downward.

The night was warm and he was bathed in sweat by the time he landed on solid footing. Ki moved toward the camp very slowly, and when a warrior appeared in the darkness, only the samurai's extraordinarily quick reflexes saved his life.

Ki's hand chopped downward and its calloused edge caught the warrior where his neck joined his shoulders. The Comanche grunted softly, and Ki caught his body and dragged it out from the camp, then returned.

There were several campfires in this canyon, but the one that interested Ki the most was that which flickered beside the large tent. It was there that he could see the Comancheros huddled around the fire beside the war chief. The girl was not with them and Ki's glance went directly toward the tent. Of course. She would be inside, quite likely tied or at least guarded.

Ki focused all his attention on the big tent. If he attempted to get to the girl now, he would be running a severe risk since the war chief would be coming to bed soon. But it was either that, or move much later and allow the Mexican girl to be used again. Furthermore, there was no guarantee that she wouldn't awake screaming, and then the entire camp would land on him.

Ki, his black hood pulled down tight over his face, moved low and fast toward the tent. When he reached the back of it, he knelt beside the canvas for several moments, listening but hearing nothing from within.

The warriors and the Comancheros were not more than fifty feet from where he knelt and Ki knew that they might decide to adjourn their conversation at any moment. There was no time to waste so he removed his bow and quiver and set them aside. Next, he withdrew his *tanto* knife from its sheath, pushed its sharp blade through the canvas, and made a long, swift incision.

Ki was starting to push his shoulders through the opening in the tent when an old woman with a leather quirt shrieked and then began to flog his hood. Ki shoved on through the canvas, battled the woman aside, and grabbed for the Mexican girl.

She jumped back and when Ki attempted to grab her again, the old woman quirted him across the eyes. Momentarily blinded, Ki struck out and knocked the woman flying. The next thing he knew, the tent was collapsing all around him. The Mexican girl was screaming and the old woman was still tearing off his hood and whipping his face.

Ki tried to escape but the tent was too big and heavy to allow him to move with any speed. By the time he cleared his stinging eyes and found the opening, he was doomed. The war chief was standing over Ki with a rifle and Ki froze.

Harsh, guttural words were spoken in the Comanche tongue, none of which Ki understood. The big Comanchero leader kicked out with his boot and it struck Ki in the face. Ki grabbed the man's leg and twisted it hard. The Comanchero cursed and fell. Ki got in one bone-crunching strike that hit the Comanchero in the neck and he would have killed the man except that someone brought a rifle barrel crashing down on his skull.

When Ki awoke, he found himself on his belly, bound hand and foot, arms pulled almost together. It was a very painful position, and that, coupled with the fact that his face was numb and covered with dried blood told him that he was in a desperate fix.

The samurai tried to roll over on his side, confident that he could somehow use his teeth to pull a hidden star blade from his costume. But he had not reckoned on a guard being close. The guard, a slender pock-faced man in his thirties, booted Ki in the ribs hard enough to knock the wind from his lungs. The samurai closed his eyes again and pretended to lose consciousness.

It was a long, painful night and it wasn't until the sun was lifting off the eastern horizon that someone threw a pail of water on his face and nudged him roughly with the toe of their boot.

"Wake up!"

Ki opened his eyes to stare upward at the Comancheros and several Indians. The big Comanchero had a nasty bruise on his face and Ki took some little satisfaction in knowing he was responsible.

"Who the hell are you!"

"I am . . . a samurai," Ki said simply.

"A what!"

"A samurai warrior."

"Well," the Comanchero said with contempt, "if I had my say, you'd be a dead warrior."

The Indian leader who'd bought the Mexican girl held Ki's bow and quiver of arrows out before him. In halting English, he said, "How shoot?"

"I'd have to demonstrate or you'd never believe me," Ki said.

The chief studied Ki very closely. "Untie," he grunted.

"Now just a minute, Gray Wolf," the big Comanchero said. "I think we need to ask this yellow sonofabitch a few questions."

Gray Wolf shook his head and one of his own warriors bent and cut the bonds that held the samurai. The rope had been so tight that the sudden rush of blood into Ki's hands and feet caused him excruciating pain but he didn't let it show.

"Up!" the Indian chief ordered.

Ki hoped that he could stand without help. Clenching his teeth, he slowly climbed to his feet.

31

"You shoot," Gray Wolf grunted.

"Shoot what?"

The chief turned and looked around for a moment, then raised his hand and pointed toward a gourd hanging from a tree. "You shoot that!"

It wasn't a request and Ki did not even want to consider what he would do if he missed. Taking his bow and quiver, the samurai selected a plain hunting arrow. He nocked it and managed to step out from the group without faltering too badly. Ki felt weak and dizzy, but he took several deep breaths and, as the entire encampment watched, he drew his bowstring back to his ear.

For a long beat, Ki held the string, feeling the pull of the bow on his muscles even as his mind grew calm and assured. It did not escape notice from the Indians that Ki's arm and hand were rock-steady. And although most of these Indians now used the white man's guns and rifles, nearly all of them had first become skilled with their traditional weapons, primary among them being the bow and arrow.

Ki did not consciously aim his arrow, but allowed his mind to leap ahead a fraction in time and actually *see* the arrow in its trajectory and then how it shattered the water gourd. When this vision was perfectly focused in his mind, he released the string, the twang of the hemp bowstring was soft, and the bow itself turned a complete half-circle so that it was now pointing at him.

The Comanche were so stunned by the bow's turning a full one hundred and eighty degrees that it was a moment before they looked back to see the broken gourd impaled by Ki's hunting arrow.

The Indians murmured with astonishment. One, still disbelieving, went to the hanging gourd and actually pulled the samurai's arrow out and inspected it with skepticism.

"Hell," the Comanchero leader hissed, "I could shoot that gourd all to hell from here. What's the fuss about?"

32

In reply, the Indian leader looked at Ki and said, "You warrior?"

"Yes," Ki said, nodding his head.

"Me warrior!" the Gray Wolf said, his mouth twisting down at the corners. "Maybe we fight!"

The Indian stared deeply into the samurai's eyes, trying but failing to detect fear.

"Why you come here?" Gray Wolf said at last.

Ki knew that his life depended on giving the right answer. This Indian chief would see right through an outright lie.

"For the woman," he said, his eyes flicking toward the tent. "For *my* woman."

"The hell you say!" the Comanchero growled. "I cut her man's throat only yesterday."

To emphasize his point, he used a thick forefinger to make a slash across his own throat. Gray Wolf and the other Comanche had no trouble understanding.

Gray Wolf tore the bow and arrows from Ki's fist. He drew his knife and said, "You lie!"

"No," Ki told him, his gaze unflinching and his voice very calm. "I come for woman."

"She my woman now!"

Ki took a deep breath. "No," he said loud enough for everyone in camp to hear. "She *my* woman."

Gray Wolf's knife came up to rest just under the samurai's chin and he felt its blade slice through his flesh and then he felt drops of blood fall to his chest. At the very same instant, however, Ki grabbed his bow and brought its daggerlike tip up to rest against Gray Wolf's flat belly.

The Indian chief looked down and saw that the tip of Ki's bow had also broken his skin and that the tip was sharp and hard enough to be driven up and under his rib cage to pierce his heart.

Gray Wolf almost smiled as he lowered his knife. "We talk," he said.

"Now wait a minute!" the big Comanchero said with

anger. "You're making a mistake here!"

The Indian chief did not like either the man's tone of voice or his words. Gray Wolf turned abruptly and said, "Go!"

"What!"

Gray Wolf did not deign to repeat himself and, after a moment, the Comanchero swallowed and turned away. "Let's get out of here," he said to his companion.

"Wait!"

All eyes turned to the samurai whose voice was hard with command.

"What the hell do you mean, 'wait'!" the big Comanchero swore. "I should have killed you last night!"

"I fought and killed all your men," Ki said, his voice challenging.

The Comanchero was a coarse-featured man with a wicked scar across his left cheek. Now that scar turned white and his eyes went as hard and black as obsidian. "You're lyin'!"

"I have one of your horses tied up above. A black gelding. I have no need to lie because if Gray Wolf allows it, I will also fight and kill you and the other man who raped my woman and cut the throat of her companion."

The Comanchero blinked with shock but he recovered fast. "All right, so you did visit my camp. And maybe you did kill my men. But they weren't much. I'm not afraid of you."

"Good," Gray Wolf said, "then you fight to the death."

It was a moment before the Comanchero managed to nod his head. He was taller and heavier than the samurai and no doubt a very experienced fighter. "That'd suit me right down to the ground," he hissed.

Gray Wolf really did smile now. "And if you lose, then that one dies too."

"Now wait a damn minute, Gray Wolf!" the second Comanchero cried. "I ain't going to die because of someone else. I figured I'm a man same as you and I deserve a fighting chance."

Gray Wolf looked at Ki with a question on his face. "You fight both?"

"Yes."

"Good. Eat first, fight later."

Ki nodded with relief. He had not eaten or slept in too long. "We fight when the sun goes down," he said.

"The hell with that!" the Comanchero said. "I want you right now! I'll carve you up like a Christmas turkey. I'll gut you like a deer and let you die slow."

"Yeah," the other Comanchero said, excitement building. "You can do it, Juara! I seen you use that knife of yours. Look at him! He ain't no match for men like you and me!"

Ki's response was to stare impassively at both men until their crowing was over. The second Comanchero was simply trying to mask his fear. He did not want to fight. He was desperately hoping that Juara would do the killing work for him.

Gray Wolf raised his hand and pointed about halfway up from the earth. "When sun reaches there," he said, "you fight."

Ki saw that the Indian chief meant that they would fight in the midafternoon during the very hottest time of day. That was all right. It would give him time to eat, wash in the spring's pond, and then take a long, long nap. He would be prepared then and he would be ready to fight to the death.

After that—if he won—he would worry about escaping with the Mexican girl.

★

Chapter 5

When Ki was awakened, the sun had slipped well past its zenith and the temperature was in the upper nineties. Even so, he felt much better because he'd eaten, washed, and then napped for nearly four hours. True, his muscles were stiff and his face was swollen but those were inconsequential discomforts that the samurai did not dwell upon.

As soon as he was fully awake, Ki did a quick series of stretching exercises which loosened his muscles. All the while, Gray Wolf watched him in silence and when Ki removed the upper part of his silk *ninja* costume, the chief and several of the warriors were surprised to see how the samurai's body rippled with smooth, sleek muscle.

Juara had also stripped down to his pants and he was impressive with his size and bulk. Because the Comanchero leader was far deeper in the chest and possessed a blacksmith's arms, Ki knew it would be foolish to attempt to match his brute strength.

No matter, Ki thought, it is always better to match speed, intelligence, reflexes, and quickness against raw physical power.

Ki and the big Comanchero were led by the Indian warriors to a circle drawn in the dirt and a squaw brought the Mexican girl to watch. When Ki's gaze matched hers, he knew that she understood he was fighting for her. But since the samurai was a stranger, it was understandable that the Mexican girl showed no interest. Her dark, heavily lidded eyes surveyed him without interest, only suspicion.

"Can I speak with her for a moment alone?" Ki asked the Indian chief.

Gray Wolf nodded.

Ki went to the girl and despite the Comanchero's angry protestations, he led her off to the edge of the camp where they could converse in private. "My Spanish," he began, "is very poor."

"Then speak to me in English, señor."

Ki blinked. "I thought . . ."

"Who are you?" she demanded. "We have never met before and even if you win this fight—which you won't—I would never be your woman."

"Look," Ki said, "I was scouting for water when I saw the Comanchero camp and then saw them kill your husband and rape you."

Tears welled up unbidden in her dark eyes and her voice took on a bitter edge. "So maybe you thought I looked good and wanted some for yourself, eh, señor!"

"No," Ki said quietly. "I saw your beauty, that is true. But also, I saw your courage—and that of your friend."

"Miguel was very brave. Too brave."

"I killed the other Comancheros," Ki said quite simply. "And I will kill these as well."

She did not believe him. Ki could see that much but it did not matter.

"Señor," she said, her shoulders suddenly sagging with defeat. "It does not matter what happens in that circle of death. Even if you win, you will lose."

"You're saying that Gray Wolf will keep both you and the money he paid Juara?"

"Yes. Gray Wolf admires courage, but not enough to give you your life. If you win the fight, Gray Wolf will torture you to see how brave you really are."

Ki had considered this a very real possibility. "Maybe if I do not cry out then . . ."

She raised her hand for silence. "And so what?" she asked in a whisper. "So what if Gray Wolf spares your life after you have been blinded, scarred, and broken? Will you want to live, half a man?"

"I don't know," Ki said. "I live by a code of honor. I could not have left you in the hands of these men and had any respect for myself. And if a man loses his own respect, then he has nothing."

"And a woman? What if a woman who has been raped, beaten, and made to do all manner of things to those animals loses *her* respect? What then?"

Ki expelled a deep breath. She was waiting for an answer—some kind of answer, any kind of answer. He could actually see her leaning forward, the faintest of hope in her eyes.

Ki reached out and his thumb brushed at her wet cheek. "You won my respect from that day to this. That is why I had to come. And if that tent had not fallen on my head, I would have gotten you out of this canyon."

She snorted, but it was not so much from derision as simply disbelief. "I have never met a man like you before. What is your name?"

"Ki."

"Mine is Donita Miller. My father was an El Paso badman who escaped across the border into Mexico. He was very brave but a little crazy."

"So it is because of him that you can speak English."

"Yes. I am a halfbreed."

38

"So am I," the samurai said, "half American, half Japanese. Like your father, my father was brave. He was a seaman and he died before I knew him."

Donita's lips curved into the merest suggestion of a smile. "That one you fight now, kill him slow. For me?"

But Ki shook his head. "I fight to win and I take no pleasure in it. If he begs for his life, it will be given him."

"Even after what he did to Miguel and myself!"

"Yes."

Her smile was replaced by a look of hurt and anger. She started to turn away, but Ki grabbed her by the arm, swung her back around, and then kissed her mouth. She struggled and he could hear the Indians snicker until her body yielded for an instant and then he pushed her away.

Her eyes flashed with anger and she would have raked him with her claws if he had not said, "If I win, they need to understand that you are my woman. It is our only hope."

"You fool! There is no hope. Gray Wolf will keep me as his woman and he will keep the Comanchero's scalp as well as your scalp and all the horses, guns, and money."

"We'll see," Ki said as he turned and walked back through the Indians to the twenty-foot circle.

Across the circle, Juara stood barefooted and bare chested. In his big right hand was an oversized bowie knife that looked to be almost as big as a machete. In Ki's hand was his own *tanto* knife. Light, thin, very, very sharp.

Juara saw the knife too and it made him laugh outright. "You gonna pick your teeth with that little thing, or what?"

Ki stepped into the circle and said, "I'm going to kill you or make you beg for your life."

"Git him!" the second Comanchero cried. "Quarter the bastard!"

39

Ki bent his knees and went into a crouch as the Comanchero came gliding smoothly across the ring with a big, hungry smile on his face.

They circled to the right, eyes locked. Ki feinted a strike but the Comanchero did not react. He had obviously done this many times before.

"Who the hell are you, anyway?" Juara hissed.

Ki did not answer. He had seen knife fighters in action more often than he cared to remember. One of their favorite tactics was to break their opponent's concentration with taunts or even idle conversation.

Juara lunged and his huge bowie knife sliced so much air that Ki felt its movement. The samurai ducked under the man's heavily muscled arm and drove his own blade across Juara's ribs, opening flesh to the bone.

Juara did not make a sound, but when they whirled about to face each other, the Comanchero's confident smile was missing. The Indians began to murmur to each other.

"Gut him!" the second Comanchero cried. "Don't let him get away with doin' that!"

Ki waited. He had been taught that patience was a great virtue and that impatient men were the ones who usually made the first crucial mistake.

"Come on!" Juara challenged. "Show some guts!"

But Ki continued to wait until Juara's beefy face grew red with anger and he advanced, the big knife cutting at the air before him. "Stick that little sonofabitch out there and I'll show you a real man's knife."

Ki knew better than to be goaded into taking such a foolish challenge. His *tanto* blade was of tempered steel, but it was no match for the far heavier bowie blade.

Suddenly, Juara jumped forward, the big knife swiftly cutting at Ki's chest. Ki jumped back and as Juara came in, drove his knife at the man's belly. They closed and when Juara threw him off, Ki saw that they had both scored across the midsection and were bleeding heavily.

Juara seemed pleased to have finally drawn blood. Bolder now, he came in slashing, kicking, and cursing.

He was not reckless but very skilled, and his charge and sparring were so fierce that it was all Ki could do with his much smaller knife to keep from being ripped to shreds. Around and around the circle they went, Ki backing up, Juara, eyes black with an insane gleam, huge knife blade dripping blood.

"Come on and close with me!" Juara bellowed when he had to stop a moment and gulp for breath. His barrel chest worked like a bellows and Ki's blade had left it bleeding in half a dozen places. For his own part, Ki was also bleeding from several wounds. One of the worst was a deep cut under his left arm that had just missed an artery.

But despite the blood, Ki was barely winded. Now he began to stalk the much larger man.

"Come on, Juara! Don't let him . . . oh, Jeezus!"

Ki's blade cut at the Comanchero so fast that it was a blur and Juara retreated fast. He was badly winded and, for the first time, Ki could see real fear in his eyes.

"Why don't you stand and fight!" the Comanchero cried in frustration. "Why don't you fight me man to man!"

"I will," Ki said softly, "just as soon as I am warmed up."

Juara opened his mouth to say something, then snapped it shut. He licked his lips and glanced down at himself and what he saw was not pretty. He was bleeding heavily.

The Comanchero planted his feet. "I ain't movin' forward or backward," he panted, "so you just come and get a taste of my steel."

"You can beg for your life and I'll give it to you," Ki offered. "You have shown your courage."

"Ha! I beg and I'm a dead man for sure! Come on! Close with me!"

Ki paused for several seconds. He could not afford to allow this man to catch his breath. There was no choice but to go straight at him.

41

Ki feinted a thrust and Juara went for it. Ki feinted again and then he really did strike for the Comanchero's belly.

But Juara deliberately stuck his left arm into the path of Ki's blade. The big man grunted with pain when the *tanto* blade cut through his forearm muscle but he retained enough presence of mind to twist his arm sideways and he locked Ki's blade between the bones of his forearm.

In desperation, Ki tried to tear his blade free, but Juara threw his arm up and he had the *tanto* blade.

Pale, but wearing a terrible smile, Juara said, "Now we'll have some fun. Leave the ring and these Indians will kill and torture you in ways you can't imagine. Stay and you're mine. Take your choice!"

Ki retreated to the perimeter of the circle. Someone must have thought he was about to cross the line because he stabbed Ki in the buttocks with his knife and would have again if Gray Wolf had not shouted something Ki did not hear or understand.

The samurai set himself, knees bent slightly, hands up though slick with blood. Almost never did he use his foot or hand strikes to kill, but this time there was absolutely no room for compromise. When they next closed, one or the other of them was going to die.

"Scared?" Juara asked mockingly. "Let me see some yellow piss runnin' down those yellow legs."

Ki kept his eyes locked on Juara's eyes which would flinch at the instant he chose to attack. Come on, he thought, let's finish this fight.

Juara had Ki's knife in his left hand and his own bowie knife in his right fist. He came at the samurai with both blades and he came hard.

Ki jumped back on his left foot and with every ounce of muscle he could focus, drove his right foot over the flashing knives and into the Comanchero's throat.

There was a sickening snap as Ki whirled and a sweep kick brought the Comanchero crashing down. Ki landed on his enemy and the hard edge of his hand again chopped at Juara's thick neck. A second audible crack could be heard very distinctly within the canyon walls.

Silence followed. Even the Indians, accustomed to violence and death, seemed to hold their breath in awe. The second Comanchero was the one who finally broke the silence.

"Jeezus!" he swore. "I ain't fightin' him!"

It was the wrong thing to say. Gray Wolf barked something out and the Comanchero was seized, then hauled away screaming.

"No! All right! I'll fight him. I'll fight him!" he cried over and over until he suddenly screamed.

Ki did not want to think about the horrible death that the smaller Comanchero was about to endure. Of course, he deserved to die, but quick, like Juara.

Ki knelt on one knee to stare at the dead Comanchero. Whatever else the man had been, he'd died bravely. He'd had enough courage to trap the *tanto* blade between the bones of his forearm knowing that the pain would be almost beyond the limits of human endurance.

Gray Wolf barked another order and Juara's bloody body was hauled out of the circle. Ki retrieved his *tanto* blade and wiped it clean on his pants. He remembered Donita's grim prophecy and squared his shoulders. If it was his karma that he was to die now, then he would do so as a warrior and he would take Gray Wolf with him to the other side.

★

Chapter 6

When Jessie had first seen Ki's pinto come trotting over a hill toward her herd, she'd felt a stab of fear go through her heart. Now, however, as dawn seeped across the grassy valley and she stared at the trail leading north, she felt much calmer.

Behind her, buried under the cottonwood trees, rested the bodies of four Comancheros. Ahead of her, she watched as Bob Hanes and Pete Willis remounted their horses and came galloping back with an early report.

"There were four horses traveling out of here to the north," Willis said.

"Shod?"

"That's right. It seems a pretty fair bet that Ki was riding one of them."

"How long ago?"

"Couple of days at least."

Jessie looked out at her herd. The cattle were devouring the grass like locusts. This was the best feed they'd had in a long, long time, and it might be the best they'd have all the way to Kansas.

"I want to hold the cattle right here for a couple of days," she decided. "They'll take this grass down pretty fast. Two. Three days at the most. They'll need what it can give them for the trip ahead."

"Yes, ma'am," the cowboys said.

"I'll take Pete Willis and we'll ride north and try to overtake Ki." The pair of cowboys made it obvious from their expressions that they didn't like this idea one bit.

Hanes said, "Miss Starbuck, I sure don't want to cross you but it ain't safe out here with just one or two men. This country is overrun with Comancheros and Indians. We'd sure rather you stayed with the herd and let us go out lookin' for the samurai."

"I know you would, but it's something I have to do." Jessie patted her palomino on his shoulder. "Besides, if I meet up with more trouble than I can handle, I feel pretty sure that I can outrun it back to help. One of the reasons I want to take Pete, besides the fact that he's a dead shot with his rifle, is that he has an extremely fast and strong horse to ride."

"But . . ."

Jessie cut Hanes off. "Bob, I appreciate your worry, but I'm leaving as soon as I can saddle my horse and ready a few provisions in case we'll be out a few days."

"Yes ma'am," Hanes said. "So we just sit here and wait?"

"No. Keep the cattle here until the grass is gone, then make sure the water barrels that old Scotty is carrying in the chuckwagon are full before you strike out for the north. But with any luck at all, Ki and I will return before then."

"Yes, ma'am."

Jessie turned and strode back to the wagon where she finished her coffee and then tossed the dregs into the grass before packing a hunk of dried beef and some dried apples into a sack. She told the crew of her plans and several other cowboys offered to take her place but she patiently declined.

"We'll be fine," she said, going out to catch up her horse, but discovering that Sonny Lane had already saddled and bridled the animal.

"You'll spoil me doing things like that," she said.

"Spoilin' you on a regular basis would be my life's greatest pleasure," Sonny said with a wide grin and just a hint of boldness in his eyes. "That, and coming along with you."

"I think Pete is enough."

"Maybe, maybe not. I'm a better shot, though."

"Is that a fact?"

"Yes, ma'am. We had a little turkey shoot last fall and I won. I'm pretty fair with a sixgun, too."

Jessie shook her head. "You sure aren't long on modesty, are you."

"No, ma'am," Sonny told her. "My mother once told me that a body has to blow their own horn 'cause no one else ever will. And I am mighty good with firearms. I come from Kentucky stock and there are no finer shots in the world, Miss Starbuck. All my kin can shoot the eyes out of squirrel at a hundred yards."

"Can you?"

He smiled boyishly. "I can do it at *two* hundred yards."

Jessie had to laugh. "All right then, come along with us."

Sonny Lane dipped his square chin with appreciation. "I sure am glad to do that, Miss Starbuck. Yes, ma'am!"

Before he turned and started for his horse, Sonny's blue eyes rested for an instant on Jessie's bosom and she felt her cheeks warm. But, again, before she could react, he was striding off to get ready to ride out and protect her life.

46

To hell with a lecture, Jessie thought, you can't get angry with a man that good-looking who just wants to save your scalp.

At that moment their cook, Scotty Duggan, limped up and stuffed a brown package into her saddlebags.

"What's that?"

"Little treat," Scotty said. "Gingersnap cookies. I figure that, if the Indians jump you, you can always toss them cookies out and them red devils won't be able to ride on they'll be so excited by the smell."

Jessie laughed and inhaled deeply. The cookies smelled wonderful. "Sounds like it'll work for certain," she said, mounting her horse.

A few moments later, she, Sonny Lane, and Pete Willis were waving goodbye to the Circle Star crew and galloping north.

The sun was scorching hot long before noon, but Jessie scarcely noticed as she kept her eyes glued to the tracks they followed. In the late afternoon they saw pine-covered mountains off in the distance.

"Tracks are leading straight to 'em," Lane said.

Jessie frowned. She did not dare ride too close because if Ki was in trouble up ahead, she and her two men needed the element of surprise. And yet, she felt that time was of the essence.

"Let's go on a little farther," she decided out loud.

A mile ahead, Jessie saw that a single horse track had peeled away from the others.

"My guess is that Ki was riding this animal," Willis said, dismounting and studying the hoofprints very intently. "As you can see, these tracks look to be a little fresher and, in places, they cover the other three, meaning this horse came along behind."

Jessie couldn't see but she nodded with agreement because Pete Willis was an excellent tracker. "Let's follow the lone horse and see where the trail leads."

Pete remounted, and they followed the lone horse for several miles until it became obvious that the rider had deliberately circled the mountains just ahead.

"See the mouth of that canyon up yonder?" Sonny Lane asked.

"Yes." Jessie had to squint because of the sun's glare and the distance.

"I got a feeling there's big trouble in that canyon. Looks to me like a trap."

"Is that a hunch or an observation?" Jessie asked.

"A hunch," Sonny told her. "I just don't like the looks of it."

"I guess Ki didn't either," Jessie said. "Let's go. It'll be dark in another hour."

By the time they reached a high plateau, it was dark, but the moonlight filtered down through the pines giving them plenty of light to follow the tracks.

"Look!"

Jessie turned her head and saw what Pete Willis was pointing toward. "It's a saddled horse!"

All three of them drew their guns and Jessie motioned for them to dismount.

The horse appeared to have been tied for a long time and it was desperate for food and water. Because there was nothing for the horse to drink, Jessie emptied most of her canteen into her hat and gave it to the thirsty animal.

"Here are the samurai's footprints," Pete said, kneeling close to the ground. "Looks like he left this horse and went toward the rim of the canyon for a look-see."

Jessie nodded, her face grim. "Let's do the same."

Ten minutes later, they were flat on their bellies looking down into the Comanche camp from the same vantage point that Ki had used.

"Holy Moses!" Willis exclaimed. "There's a bunch of them down there."

"All I want to see is Ki," Jessie said, trying but failing to hide her growing anxiety.

They all stared down into the Comanche canyon but even though the moonlight was full, it was not sufficient to see across a long distance with any real clarity.

48

"He's got to be down there," Sonny said hopefully. "The question we have to ask is, can Ki still be alive?"

"Of course he can," Jessie said with more conviction than she really felt.

Pete growled. "Miss Starbuck, the thing that I can't understand is why he'd have gone down there in the first place."

"It seems obvious to me that only one thing would make him go in there and that would be to rescue someone," Jessie said. "Otherwise, he'd have stayed far away from a trap like this."

There was a long silence and then Sonny said, "So what do you want to do, Miss Starbuck?"

"We have to go down and find Ki and then bring him out alive."

Pete and Sonny exchanged worried glances. Pete said, "Miss Starbuck, the light is bad but from what I can see, these canyon walls are mighty steep and I doubt very much we could get down to the canyon floor."

"He's right," Sonny agreed. "And even if we could, we'd never get back up the walls. Not alive, at least."

"Well we can't just sit here and wait!" Jessie exclaimed. "Come daylight, we'd have no chance at all of sneaking through that camp."

"What makes you think we'd have one now?"

Jessie edged back from the rim and stood up. She started back toward the horses.

"What are you going to do!" Sonny whispered.

"We have three good ropes," Jessie told him. "And even if they won't quite reach the canyon floor, they'll go most of the way. I mean to enter that camp tonight and find Ki if he's in there still alive."

Jessie marched to the horses and removed all three ropes, but before she could tie them together, Sonny took them from her hands.

"Hell," he grunted, "I'll go down there."

"No," Jessie said. "It's too risky. Ki is my best friend. I'm the one that ought to go."

"But I'm the best man for the job!"

"And I'm the best woman!" Jessie stomped her boot on the hard earth. "And furthermore, I'm your boss!"

Sonny mockingly stomped his own boot. "Then I'll quit on you right now because you're not going down into that canyon."

"You are a pigheaded man."

"And you're a pigheaded woman," he said, stomping off toward the rim of the canyon.

Jessie went after him, angry as hell. "I don't see why I can't go down there just as well as you can," she hissed as Sonny tied the three ropes together, then anchored them around the trunk of a pine tree.

"The reason is that you're not as strong as me and you weren't raised in the woods hunting like I was. If you were and if I thought you'd have any chance at all of getting down there and into that Indian camp, believe me, I'd let you go."

Jessie knew that further argument would be futile and counterproductive. "All right," she said, "but if we hear gunfire, then . . ."

"Then don't do a damn thing except get on your horses and skedaddle!"

Jessie's fists knotted in anger as she stared at the big cowboy, then down at the Indian camp. "Do you have any idea where you're going to look?"

"Nope," he said. "But my guess is that the answer will be found in that tent. That's where the number one Indian will be found. He'll know if Ki is alive or dead."

"But how will you ever . . ."

Sonny Lane reached out and grabbed her around the waist, then crushed her to his chest and kissed her mouth roughly. Jessie struggled and finally broke away.

"What the hell is the matter with you!" she hissed.

Sonny grinned. "I just figure that, if I'm going to die in the next few minutes, I wanted to do that first so I won't consider this has been a total loss."

"You're crazy!"

"That goes without saying," Sonny Lane told her.

50

Jessie turned to Pete Willis who had a stupid grin on his round face. "What are you grinning about!"

The grin died. "Not a thing, Miss Starbuck."

Pete stuck his hand out and shook Sonny's hand. "If we never see you again, it's been fun. And I won't miss you the next time we have another turkey shoot and I place first."

"I'll just bet you won't," Sonny said as he took the rope and started over the side.

★

Chapter 7

Sonny Lane had fashioned a sling with his belt to strap his Winchester carbine across his back, but the damned thing had slipped around so that it was hanging under his belly. He could hear Jessie and Pete Willis up above letting out rope and whispering encouragement down to him. Sonny wished they'd just be quiet.

Sonny wasn't a hero and he hadn't wanted to go over the side of this canyon, but he couldn't let Jessie do it and, besides, if the samurai was man enough to descend this cliff, then so was he.

He hoped.

The cliff was incredibly smooth and there were damn few hand or footholds. In the moonlight, he could see where the samurai had used every irregularity he could find in the rock as well as the bushes he'd used to hang onto. But the samurai had not even had a rope. Several times, Sonny lost his grip on the wall and he knew that he'd have fallen if it hadn't been for the rope.

Still fifteen or twenty feet from the canyon floor, the rope played out and Sonny reached inside his belt for his bowie knife. Setting his feet on a thick ledge of rock, he gripped a bush and then he cut the rope loose. He tottered off-balance for a moment, then hugged the rock, his heart hammering in his chest.

Christ, he thought, how am I going to get out of this canyon before dawn? I won't even be able to reach the rope from down below.

This question troubled him so greatly that he felt beads of sweat pop out across his forehead. He was sure that he'd never been in a worse situation. Now, he was stuck on a rock wall with no way to get down the last ten feet and with an entire camp of murdering Indians less than a quarter mile away.

For almost five minutes, Sonny clung to the rock and then, since he could think of no better solution and he knew he could spend all his strength just clinging to the rock, he kicked out and tried to twist like a cat as he fell.

Roll! he told himself. Hit the ground and roll!

But when he hit the canyon floor, two things went terribly wrong—he almost impaled himself on the damned Winchester, and he badly twisted his right ankle.

It was all that Sonny Lane could do to keep from crying out in pain as he writhed in sheer agony for the next few minutes. The butt of the rifle had punched in under his ribs and knocked him breathless and it felt as if he'd separated his ribs.

The ankle was a fire that sent waves of flame up and down his entire right leg. Sonny reached out and clasped the ankle in his hands as he rocked back and forth, gritting his teeth against the pain.

From up above, Jessie could see Sonny and she knew something was very wrong.

"Pull the rope up, quick!"

Pete Willis did as he was told. The rope came up fast and when Jessie grabbed its end, she began to tie it around her waist.

"What are you going to do!" Willis hissed in near panic.

"Look at him," Jessie said. "He's hurt. I can't leave him like that!"

"But . . ."

"Let me down slow," Jessie said, leaving her own rifle and relying instead on her sixgun. "Just let me down and then wait. If you see that we won't be coming back, gather those horses and get back to the herd to warn them what happened."

"I can't leave you down there!"

"You can't help us by getting yourself killed," Jessie said as she started over the rim.

Jessie was light enough so that Willis could almost lower her down the wall much faster than Sonny. When she reached the end of her rope, she was at least twenty feet from the canyon floor, but her smaller fingers and feet were able to find purchase on the rock. Cutting herself free of the rope, she was able to descend almost to the floor before she jumped.

"Dammit!" Sonny hissed, still clutching his ankle. "Now you've written your death warrant the same as mine."

"Not quite," Jessie said, kneeling beside the big cowboy. "Is it broken?"

"No," Sonny grunted, "but it couldn't hurt any worse if it was."

"Just stay here by the wall," Jessie said. "I'm going to find Ki. If he's still alive, he'll be able to help us out of this mess."

Sonny shook his head with dejection. "I sure messed this up, didn't I."

"You're a cowboy, not a circus acrobat," Jessie said. "And you're a brave man."

"You want my rifle?"

"No. If I have to use it, we're finished anyway."

"Good luck, Jessie. I can call you that since I quit working for you up above."

"You earned that right simply by volunteering to come down here," Jessie said as she slipped away in the moonlight.

Jessie removed her Stetson and headed for the big tent, which seemed to be the center of the camp. It was probably after midnight and as she neared the perimeter of the Comanche camp she could see that a few fires were burning, but everyone seemed to be asleep. Jessie came upon a sleeping warrior and she carefully removed an old army blanket that had been tossed aside in the warm night air.

Wrapping the blanket around herself, she crept toward the big tent, passing around more and more sleeping Indians. Suddenly, one grunted, rolled to his feet and staggered over to the edge of the camp. Jessie dropped to the earth and watched as the Indian urinated on the grass, then came stumbling back to his place where he returned to sleep.

Somehow, she reached the big tent and she was just about to go inside when something stopped her dead in her tracks.

"Pssst! Pssst!"

Jessie turned to see Ki hog-tied only a few yards away. She almost cried out with happiness before she hurried over to the samurai and cut his ropes away.

Ki pulled her face close to his and whispered, "How did you get here!"

"Same way as you. Let's go!"

But for reasons she could not even begin to imagine, he shook his head and whispered, "Lie down. Cover yourself and those ropes with the blanket and do not move until I come back."

Jessie bit back a protest. Everything in her wanted to argue this course of action. It was going to require all of the samurai's skill and ingenuity to get them out of this canyon and up the wall. They certainly did not need to waste time now.

Ki moved into the tent whose interior was pitch black.

His eyes strained to find the Mexican girl and when he stumbled over a body, he dropped to one knee and hissed, "Donita?"

Gray Wolf started out of sleep and even though Ki could not see the war chief's face, he knew that the Comanche was going to shout. Ki's hand chopped down blindly. It struck Gray Wolf's nose and broke it with a sickening crunch. The warrior gasped and then he groped for his knife but Ki's hand was already slashing downward a second time and now the hard edge of his palm connected with the warrior's neck.

Gray Wolf grunted and went limp. Ki touched his throat and felt a pulse. Since Ki figured he would need every available minute to escape with Jessie, his thumb and forefinger dug into the Indian chief's muscular neck. Even in total darkness, Ki found the warrior's atemi point which instantly dammed the flow of arterial blood to the Indian's brain. Gray Wolf sank even deeper into unconsciousness until Ki removed his finger and thumb from the pressure point.

"Donita?" he whispered.

"Ki!"

He knelt and found the Mexican woman just beyond Gray Wolf's body. "It is time to escape," he whispered. "Don't say anything."

The girl had real presence of mind. She grabbed and clutched Ki's hand with all of her strength and he helped her to stand, then led her outside to Jessie.

"Let's go," he whispered.

"Now I see why you wanted to go back inside that tent," Jessie said in a soft voice.

Donita had been naked in the tent and Ki had been so preoccupied with Gray Wolf that he hadn't even noticed until now.

"Here," Jessie said, giving her blanket to the girl. "Wrap this around you."

"I have a dress inside."

Ki went back inside and found the woman's dress as well as his weapons. With his *tanto* blade and bow as

56

well as quiver of arrows, he suddenly felt much, much better.

Donita slipped her ragged dress on and Jessie helped her with the bone buttons. A moment later, Ki was leading them through the sleeping camp toward the cliff where they had descended.

"Well I'll be damned!" Sonny exclaimed when they came upon him. "I wouldn't have given long odds on seeing any of you again."

In a glance, the samurai understood the grim circumstances. He craned his head back and looked up the rock wall toward Pete Willis, who seemed very, very far above him.

"We've got to get the rope down here so you can tie it around your waists and then we'll have the horses pull you up."

"But how!"

Ki was so concentrated on getting up to the rope that he did not hear the question. Instead, he backed up, spied a little protrusion on the rock about five feet up and jumped for it. His foot landed on the protrusion of rock and his powerful leg propelled him up so that he was able to snap his hand on the rope.

The rest was easy enough. Scrabbling and clawing, using Pete's help from up above, Ki quickly scaled the canyon wall.

"I don't know how you did that!" Pete exclaimed.

"It doesn't matter. We need to bring the horses over here. Quickly."

Five minutes later, they did have the horses ready. Ki cut the thick leather reins from the Comanchero's horse and tied them together securely.

"Draw up the rope!"

Pete did not ask any more questions and when Ki extended the rope's length by using the reins, he quickly understood what to do and wrapped the end of the rope around a saddlehorn.

"The women first," Ki said. "I don't know if the reins are strong enough to pull Sonny up the side of that

57

canyon, but I'm not worried about Jessie or Donita."

"Who's she?"

"Never mind."

The rope and reins were tossed over the side and Donita was the first one to be pulled up the cliff by one of the horses. She was scraped and battered but otherwise unhurt.

Jessie was next and when she cleared the rim, she was panting and clawing. "Do you think that those leather reins will take his weight?"

"I don't know," Ki admitted. "But we're about to find out."

They threw the line down once more and watched as Sonny limped to grab it, then tie it around his cartridge belt.

Pete Willis had dallied the rope around Jessie's own saddlehorn and when the signal was given, the tall palomino's hooves scrambled like crazy as it struggled to pull the big cowboy up and out of the Comanchero canyon.

"Grab his other arm!" Ki ordered as soon as Sonny's head cleared the rim. The cowboy was gasping in pain and it took both Ki and Pete to drag him over the rim.

For almost a minute, they just lay there on the pine-dotted plateau gasping for air. Finally, Ki looked down at the canyon.

"It isn't over," he said. "Maybe I should have killed Gray Wolf, but I didn't. I expect that he'll come up here looking for us. Failing that, he'll pick up our tracks and follow us to the herd."

"Maybe we could wipe out our tracks," Sonny grunted.

"No," Willis said. "We'd just waste a lot of precious time for nothing."

"He's right," the samurai said. "The best thing that we can do now is to reach the herd."

"But how many men do you have?" Donita asked, her black eyes round with fear as she gazed down at the hated Comanche camp. "Surely it is not enough to stop so many."

58

"No," Jessie said, "not as many as them. But my cowboys are fighters. If we know that these Indians will come for you and the rest of us, we'll have a good chance."

"*Your* cowboys?" Donita asked.

"I'll explain some other time," Jessie said, untying the rope from her saddlehorn and stroking the trembling palomino as she told it what a fine job it had done to pull up Sonny Lane.

Just minutes later, they were mounted. Because the Comanchero horse Ki had used was thin and weak from lack of food and water, they put Donita on its back. Ki rode double behind Jessie on Sun.

"Only about two hours until dawn," Jessie said, glancing up at the fading stars. "And it will take us at least an hour to loop around these mountains."

"Then let's go," Ki said, drumming his heels against Sun's golden flanks.

They rode away quickly. If they could reach the trail herd before the Comanche overtook them, they would have a chance—but if not . . . well, they did not even want to consider that grim possibility.

★

Chapter 8

Jessie hated to see the sunrise. The sunrise would bring the Comanche on their swift war horses. After two hours of hard traveling, it had become obvious that the Comanchero horse that Ki had left on the plateau was not strong enough to keep up a fast pace.

"If we run him any more, it will kill him," Pete Willis called.

Jessie reined in her palomino and turned back to the samurai. "We'll put the girl behind Pete and leave that horse for the Comanche to find."

The switch was quickly made and now two of their horses were riding double as they pushed south.

By noon, they could see that the Comanche were on their trail and within two hours, Jessie and Ki both knew that there was no chance of outrunning their pursuers.

"I'll make a stand," Ki said urgently. "Pull in your horse and I'll make a stand."

"No!" Jessie cried. "We'll all make a stand except the girl. She can take my horse and run for help. The Comancheros' old camp where the herd is grazing can't be too much farther."

Ki was not sure. He had ridden much of this hard land during the darkness and so the landmarks were missing for him. And he would have argued this plan except that he knew the Comanche would simply flank him in this open country and quickly overtake Jessie. She was right, they had to all make a stand.

"Over there," Ki said, pointing across Jessie's shoulder to a rocky hillock that would at least afford some protection. "That's the best that we can do."

Jessie agreed and so they raced on to the hillock. Their horses were heavily lathered and plunging about in fear as the samurai threw Donita on Jessie's horse.

"Ride that way!" he commanded, pointing due south. "They can't overtake this horse so keep him moving but don't break his wind and watch out for prairie dog holes so you don't break his legs. I don't have to tell you what will happen if the Comanche overtake you before you reach the herd."

The halfbreed girl from below the border nodded, her lovely face pale except for the dark bruises on her neck and around her mouth. Ki knew that Gray Wolf had treated her brutally as his new acquisition. The big Comanche war chief would not have been a tender or a considerate lover and Donita would have fought him with all her strength.

Donita looked back at the charging Indians. They appeared invincible and she recognized Gray Wolf in their lead.

"They will overrun and kill you all. If they take you alive . . ."

"They won't," Ki said quickly. "Now ride!"

The samurai boxed Sun across the rump and the tall palomino jumped away and raced south with the girl

61

hanging onto Jessie's saddlehorn for dear life.

Ki unhooked his bow from behind his back and grabbed an arrow. There were six left and he knew that he would make every one count.

"What I wouldn't give for a buffalo rifle," Sonny Lane swore. "I'd just lay its big old barrel across this rock and take aim on that chief and I'd blow a hole in his chest bigger than a tin plate."

"Just be thankful that we've got Winchesters and not just pistols," Jessie said, levering a shell into the chamber of her rifle and hunkering down low behind her cover.

Pete Willis looked up at the sun. "It's a good day to die, I reckon."

"This isn't over yet," the samurai told him. "Not yet."

Jessie glanced sideways at Sonny. "I let you come along because you said you were the best marksman on my payroll. It's time to prove it."

"He said that!" Pete Willis cried with mock indignation. "Well we'll just see about that!"

"Hold your fire," Jessie said, "until I give the order to shoot."

She raised her hand and held it aloft until the Indians were clearly in firing range and then she said, "Fire!"

Sonny's rifle was the first to buck and Gray Wolf's horse did a somersault. Jessie saw the chief fly over the animal's head and the Comanche somehow managed to land on his feet as his warriors swept toward the hillock.

Their rifles belched smoke, fire, and lead and before the Comanche could overrun them, six horses passed by riderless. Two Indians, however, peeled off around the hillock and went racing south.

"Get them!" Jessie shouted. "They're after Donita!"

But the Indians were too far out of rifle range and when they turned back to fire, they all saw one of Ki's arrows lift a Comanche from the back of his horse and send him tumbling to the earth.

The Comanche charge broke in the face of the murderous fire that Jessie and her friends laid down from the slight elevation of their hillock. The Indians pulled back and Ki saw Gray Wolf angrily shouting and gesturing to his warriors.

"What are they going to do now?" Sonny asked.

"Watch their chief," Jessie said. "That'll be the first clue."

Gray Wolf had one of his warriors catch up with a riderless horse. He mounted the animal and raised his own repeating rifle and bellowed a challenge. Then, he rode out alone and called out over and over something that they could not understand.

"What is he saying?" Jessie asked.

Ki frowned with concentration and he finally said, "I think he wants me."

"What!"

"He wants me to come out and fight him."

"To hell with that!" Jessie swore.

"If I fight him and win, then maybe we will all be free to go."

"And maybe not," Jessie argued.

"There are still more Indians than we can handle," Ki said as he stood. "And they'll come at us from out of the sun in a few hours. That is why I must go."

Jessie also came to her feet. "No," she pleaded. "If he kills you . . ."

"Then I die as he would die—a warrior. But if I kill Gray Wolf, then maybe we will all be allowed to go free."

"There's no guarantee of that!"

"No," Ki admitted, "but there is no choice but to take this gamble."

Jessie knew that Ki was right. That didn't help at all. "You can't match that big Comanche fighting on horseback. You must somehow get to him the ground."

Ki nodded. He had pretty much reached the exact same conclusion. The Comanches were superb horsemen. They had hunted and fought from the backs of their Indian ponies since early childhood. Ki, on the other hand, was a foot warrior. A man whose arsenal of

63

weapons, kicks, and strikes were effective only on the ground.

"I will go out there on foot," Ki decided.

"Against a mounted warrior!" Sonny Lane exclaimed. "That's as good as suicide!"

Ki ignored the remark as he stepped out of the rocks and strode toward the Indian.

"He left his bow and arrows!" Pete Willis cried, starting to go after the samurai.

Jessie grabbed his arm. "He left them on purpose."

"But . . ."

The words died on Pete's lips as Gray Wolf, seeing Ki had not brought his bow and arrows, threw his Winchester aside and instead selected a war lance tipped with a steel point and decorated with arrows. The chief drummed his heels into his pony's flanks and the animal jumped forward as all the Comanches howled with excitement and expectation.

Ki looked extremely vulnerable out there on foot and Jessie gripped her hands together to keep from showing her fear. As Gray Wolf's pony thundered across the withered brown grass, the chief raised his lance and emitted a high, keening sound that sent chills up and down Jessie's spine.

About fifty yards out from the rocks, Ki stopped, and although his back was to Jessie, she saw him take a deep breath and expel it slowly. Then, he spaced his feet and assumed his traditional samurai fighting position with both hands slightly raised, body half turned, the picture of perfect balance.

"That Indian will slam him down with his war horse," Sonny said. "It'll break him in half and then all the chief will need to do is dismount and finish carving his bacon."

"Don't be so sure of that," Jessie said in a voice as dry as the stricken Texas plains.

Gray Wolf lowered his lance so that the point was aimed at Ki's chest and his Comanche warriors fell into expectant silence. Other than her own pounding heartbeat, the only thing that Jessie could hear was the hooves.

The tension was broken when Gray Wolf screamed an ancient blood-curdling cry and then leaned forward just as his horse seemed to strike the samurai.

Jessie blinked. Just a blink of her eye but in that split second, she missed seeing the samurai leap up and grab the war lance and use it to tear the Comanche chief from the back of his horse.

Gray Wolf struck the earth and rolled. Jessie could not imagine how anyone could hit the ground so hard and still be able to jump to their feet but Gray Wolf proved it was possible. The chief tore a knife from his belt and the Comanche shouted with approval as he lunged at the samurai and drew a wicked slash across his chest.

Jessie heard a metallic sound and turned to see Sonny Lane lever a shell into his Winchester. "Bye, bye Indian," he whispered, laying his cheek down on the stock and taking aim.

"No!" Jessie cried, throwing herself at the rifle as it exploded.

Gray Wolf and everyone else froze for an instant as Jessie shouted, "Let them fight!"

Sonny, his pride bruised, released his rifle. "I was trying to save your protector and friend. That big Indian will carve him up alive!"

Jessie hurled the Winchester aside. "You shoot that chief and we're all finished, dammit!"

Gray Wolf and Ki turned back to fight each other. They circled warily and then Ki attacked, feet and hands striking the Indian in the stomach, the arm, and then the face.

Gray Wolf staggered and shook his head. He grinned and nodded with appreciation. Ki bent at the waist a little and waited for the attack.

Gray Wolf had seen Ki fight the big Comanchero so there were no surprises this time. Ki feinted a blow but the chief knew better than to go for it. Twice more, Ki feinted and then the Indian struck, driving his knife up toward the samurai's flat belly.

Ki grabbed the chief's wrist and the two strained against each other for a moment and then Ki threw Gray Wolf over his hip. The chief struck the ground heavily and Ki was on him in an instant, tearing his knife free and hurling it aside. He raised his hand like an ax and Jessie knew that he could have chopped the big Indian across the throat and broken his neck.

Gray Wolf stared up at the samurai's raised hand and then he relaxed and began to sing his own death song.

Ki paused a long moment, then he lowered his hand. Gray Wolf seemed to shudder and then he grabbed Ki's hand and shook it hard.

The Indians were stunned for a moment and then they lowered their weapons and shouted with approval. Gray Wolf had accepted his death but the other warrior had not. The fight was over and it had been good.

"Well I'll be damned," Sonny whispered.

Jessie sagged with relief and tears of joy burned her green eyes. "Me too," she managed to say in a voice thick with emotion. "Me too."

★
Chapter 9

The Circle Star cowboys met them several miles north of the herd and the moment that Jessie, Ki, Sonny, and Pete came riding into view, the cowboys sent up a holler that could have been heard in Mexico.

"We thought you were goners for sure by now," Bob Hanes said with a grin that looked as if it might split his face in half.

"That's right," Len chimed in. "We thought we was going to have to go it on alone all the way up to Kansas without you."

"Fortunately not," Jessie said, proud of all of them. "But we've still got a long way to go and a lot of hard trail ahead."

Donita was also with the cowboys and she had eyes only for the samurai. "You did it," she said to him alone.

Ki blushed a little. "We all did what had to be done."

Sonny cleared his throat. "I tried my damnedest to be the hero, but I twisted my damn ankle, almost run my

gut through with my own rifle, and wasn't much use at
the showdown except to almost shoot the chief and get
us all killed."

Jessie could see that the man was trying to make
light of his failure but she knew that, inside, Sonny
Lane felt hurt and humiliated because he hadn't been
very successful at helping her, Donita, or the samurai.

"You were as brave as could be," she said to the
cowboy. "I'd never fault a man for trying. As far as
I'm concerned, you're all heroes."

The cowboys hooted a little at that but Jessie could
see that her praise made a considerable difference in
restoring Sonny's spirits.

"Let's get back to the herd," Jessie said. "Is the grass
eaten down in that Comanchero valley?"

"Right down to the roots," Hanes said. "But you can
see that the rest and feed have made a big difference on
those cattle. They've all gained at least fifty pounds."

"They'll need it," Jessie said. "We'll start driving them
north again the first thing tomorrow."

Donita fell in beside Ki and boldly asked him if he
wanted to ride behind her the rest of the way back to the
trail drive.

Ki declined to the smirking amusement of the cowboys. When they arrived back at the herd, only their cook
Scotty Duggan and two other cowboys had remained to
guard the cattle.

Jessie was famished and worn out. Sonny Lane had
to be helped to his bedroll and when they got his boot
off, his ankle was the size of a melon.

"You'll ride on the wagon beside Scotty for the next
few days until that ankle heals," Jessie told him.

"No ma'am," he said.

"What does that mean?"

"It means I quit working for you and now that I can't
work, it doesn't seem right to collect pay."

Jessie shook her head. "Sonny, before this herd reaches the railhead in Kansas, you'll have earned every pen-
ny of your pay. So don't give me any more back talk.

Just eat, rest that ankle, and be ready to help out old Scotty as best you can."

Sonny laughed. "Scotty is a bear to be around all day. I guess my punishment for past sins is to be pleasant to him, huh?"

"I guess," Jessie said. "But don't you even think about quitting, at least not until this herd is loaded in boxcars and on its way to Chicago or wherever it will go. I need your skills with weapons, Sonny. I need them very much."

He blushed with pride. "I'll be ready when trouble comes again. And next time, I won't be so intent on trying to show the samurai a thing or two as I will be on protecting you and your herd."

She reached out and touched his hand. "Thanks."

Sonny nodded awkwardly and hobbled over to get himself a cup of coffee.

That night, everyone went to bed very early and Jessie was no exception. As usual, Ki chose to sleep apart from the others, out where he could hear the sounds of any approaching danger.

About midnight, Jessie awoke to see Donita slip out from her blankets close by and hurriedly pull on her dress, then tiptoe through the camp.

Jessie thought nothing of it, assuming that the young halfbreed woman simply had to relieve herself. But Donita walked out to where the samurai was sleeping and knelt at his side. She thought Ki was sound asleep until his knife flashed up to her throat.

"Uh!"

"Shh," he ordered in a whisper. "What are you doing out here at this time of night?"

She swallowed and looked down at the point of his knife. "I could talk easier if you put that away."

"Oh," Ki said, sheathing the knife. "Well?"

"I wanted to thank you for coming into the Comanche camp and saving me."

"No thanks necessary. Anyway," Ki added, "I didn't do that good of a job. Remember?"

"I remember that you almost gave your life to save mine. Why?"

"Code of honor."

"And that's all?"

"I live by a code of honor," he told her.

Donita settled in close by his side. He could smell her hair and it was the same sweet, soapy fragrance that Jessie used when she bathed. No surprise there since the girl had no doubt used Jessie's toiletries.

"Do you love her?"

"Who?" Ki asked impatiently.

"Miss Starbuck."

"No."

Donita cocked her head sideways. "How could you not? She is the most beautiful woman I've ever seen."

"Yes," Ki said agreeably, "she is very beautiful. But we are friends, not lovers."

"I don't see how that could be," Donita said. "Every man I ever knew always said he wanted to be my friend, but what he really meant was that he wanted to be my lover."

Ki had to struggle not to smile. Donita, despite some nasty bruises, was a very handsome girl, and he had seen her without clothes so that he knew she was well-endowed.

"It is sometimes hard," Ki said when she kept looking at him with a question in her eyes. "I wouldn't try and tell you that I've never thought about how it would feel to make love to Miss Starbuck."

"She would let you."

"No."

"Oh yes! I can see it in her eyes. She considers you to be her secret lover."

"That's crazy!" Ki hissed with more than a little irritation. "Jessie has her own men, I sometimes have . . ."

Ki's words died on his lips because he didn't like the look in Donita's eyes.

"Have your own woman?" she asked coyly. "Is that what you were going to say?"

"Yes."

Donita reached out and pulled off his blanket. "I want to be your woman tonight."

Ki chuckled. "After all you've been through between the Comancheros and Gray Wolf?"

"Because of all I've been through," she corrected.

"This is crazy."

She reached out and placed her hand on his crotch, then began to massage him into a hard erection. "Maybe it is," she said. "But I have never had a man risk his life for me. And who knows, tomorrow we may be killed by another band of Indians. It could happen and then I would never have had the chance to thank you."

"I didn't go into that canyon for your thanks," Ki said, discovering his voice was getting hoarse with desire. "I went in for . . ."

"Honor," she whispered, sliding her fingers into his pants and her tongue into his ear.

"Yes," Ki groaned. "Honor."

Donita's mouth found his and their tongues clashed passionately. He could hear her breathing fast and when she pulled away and began to tear her dress off, Ki figured he'd done all that he could to preserve her honor. He did not understand why she'd want a man so soon after being raped and abused, but perhaps she would feel an inner cleansing if she made love to a man she respected and admired.

Donita's chest was heaving when she threw a shapely brown leg over the samurai and squatted down to impale herself on his throbbing manhood.

"Ooh," she moaned as Ki arched his hips upward, thrusting as she began to bounce on his rod, twisting and shaking her muscular little bottom.

Ki let her work as long and as hard as she wanted. After five minutes, she was glistening with sweat, panting and groaning so loud that he was afraid that she might either wake up Jessie and the cowboys, or cause the longhorns to stampede.

71

Hell, Ki thought, what a tale it would be if the cattle stampeded over us and the cowboys found us tomorrow morning still locked in this position!

"Here," he grunted, gripping her shoulders and bringing her nipples to his mouth. He sucked on them both for several minutes and when she really began to get loud, the samurai rolled her over onto her back.

"Now," he rasped, "let's get right down to serious business."

She bit her lip and her eyelids fluttered as he began to piston in and out of her hard, clean body.

"Hurry!" she begged, her fingernails clawing at his buttocks. "Hurry!"

Ki was ready to hurry. He'd had a long, hard day and his stamina wasn't quite up to a marathon session of lovemaking so he let his control go and very quickly she milked him into a frenzy that caused him to slam his manhood in as far as it would go and fill her with his seed.

Donita also let go and he had to smother her cries with his mouth, or she would have brought the entire trailherd and its crew running over to investigate.

When they both stopped jerking spasmodically, Ki slumped down and rolled off of her, his big root still pumping even though he was dry.

"Oh, Ki," she whispered, rolling over to stare at his face, "that made me feel whole again!"

"It didn't make me feel any the less either," he admitted. "But we've got some mighty long days ahead of us."

She reached down and grabbed his wet and softening root. "And many long nights, eh?"

He had to chuckle. "I was afraid that, after everything you went through, you'd be . . ."

"What?"

"Afraid of men. Hating them. I don't know."

"Not all men," she said. "Not a man like you."

Donita climbed back onto him and, with his tool in her fist, she began to rub it against her wet bottom.

"I can't," he protested.

"I think you can," she whispered, eyes glazed with desire, body glistening in the moonlight.

Ki laced his fingers behind his head and enjoyed the sight of her beautiful body and the things that she was doing to him.

And only a few minutes later, she chuckled happily and said, "Didn't I tell you!"

Ki glanced down between their bare legs and saw, to his amazement, that he was already stiff again.

"You were right," he groaned as she sat down on his root and began to squirm like a happy hen on a nest of eggs. "You were absolutely right."

★

Chapter 10

A week had passed since their fateful confrontation with Gray Wolf and his Comanche warriors. Twice, Gray Wolf had overtaken the herd and demanded a few cattle for his warriors and Jessie had gladly met his requests. And now, she expected the chief and his warriors to continue to dog her herd north and repeat their demands.

Jessie was almost grateful. Gray Wolf had their respect and his nearness would insure that other Indians did not attack or try to stampede the herd. And if it cost her a hundred longhorns before she reached the Canadian, so what? It was a small price for the protection she had of the warrior chief and his followers.

Besides, the lack of water and grass had become Jessie's greatest concern and fear. Since leaving the Comanchero valley more than a week before, there had been little grass and far too few water holes. It was hard on the cowboys and even harder on Jessie to watch the stock suffer. Days

74

on end of travel through dry, blistered West Texas had filled their lungs with trail dust and baked their brains. Men, cattle, and horses were all red-eyed and irritable, and Jessie saw normally congenial cowboys turn cross and surly.

The one-eyed brindle bull, however, just kept plugging across the hot, dusty miles. No longer did any of the other longhorns challenge the brindle's right of supremacy.

Ki was inexhaustible in his advance search for green grass and good water and one day he came upon a huge bowl of earth with a glistening pond surrounded by many acres of grass. The sight was so beautiful and unexpected that the samurai thought he was seeing a mirage.

He galloped his horse down to the water and dismounted. His thirsty horse drank deeply as the samurai waded out into the shallow water and then collapsed and splashed about like a child.

Ki had drunk from his canteen only a few minutes before this wonderful discovery, but now he drank a little more. The water tasted good and it cooled his hot flesh.

He would have liked to have remained half-submerged in the pond for hours, so dry and hot was his skin, but he knew that was a luxury that would come later.

"We've got to get back and tell everyone about this," he told his pinto.

In answer, the pinto dipped its muzzle once more in the water and then Ki, soaking wet but with a broad smile, mounted and turned south to spread the good news.

"It's about five miles ahead!" he told Jessie in a rush, unable to maintain his usual self-control. "Enough water and green grass for two days!"

Jessie smiled so widely that her parched lips cracked. "Let's go take a good look!"

Jessie shouted for the cowboys to drive her herd faster and then she and Ki raced north. Soon, they came upon the natural basin and it was a sight that brought gladness

75

to Jessie's heart. Before her, stretched in a great bowl of land, lay a shimmering body of water. True, it was very shallow, but it covered at least a quarter acre, and the surrounding grass was lush.

Jessie beamed and rode her palomino down toward the water until something caught her eye and she said, "Look."

Off about two hundred yards to their right, half-hidden in the grass, she saw a turkey vulture flopping about. It appeared to be trying to fly but something seemed to be wrong with its limbs.

"Ki!"

The samurai was already driving his horse toward the large bird and he dismounted on the run. The vulture swung its ugly head about and actually made a hissing sound. It tried to puff itself up and after a minute, it attempted to run.

"Look," Ki said with growing dread. "Its legs are out of control, the muscles aren't working."

Ki turned to the body of water, a ball of fear growing in his belly.

Jessie said, "Are you thinking what I'm thinking?"

"I don't know. Let's scout around."

Jessie knew what they would be looking for and she hoped that they did not find any more dead or dying birds or animals in the tall grass.

But they did.

Nothing large like deer or antelope, but there were plenty of small creatures. Rabbits, mice, a weasel, and several smaller birds.

"Did you drink any of the water!" Jessie cried.

"A little. I didn't see or taste anything wrong."

Jessie groaned. "I've heard of this happening before. Sometimes the poison in the water is in such small amounts that it doesn't affect life for hours."

Ki swallowed. He was not afraid of death in battle because that was the way of a warrior. But to die of poisoning, his perfectly conditioned body convulsing and twitching in spasms like that of the turkey vulture, now that was something that filled him with an almost overwhelming dread.

Just then, Ki's horse dropped to its knees, tried to climb back to its feet and then toppled over and began to thrash.

"Oh Lord no," Jessie said. "Let's get out of here!"

"We can't just leave that poor animal like that!"

Jessie tore her rifle from its saddle boot. "You're right," she said grimly. "We can't."

Ki looked very pale as she put two bullets into the pinto's head. Maybe it was premature and they could have nursed the animal back to health, but there wasn't time to find out. Whatever was in the water was tasteless, colorless, and very deadly.

Jessie jammed her smoking Winchester back into her scabbard and quickly mounted the palomino. "Come on," she said, kicking her left boot from the stirrup. "There's no time to waste."

The samurai felt a twist in his guts that was so sharp and painful it brought a groan to his lips which he couldn't stifle.

"Hurry!" Jessie cried as Ki's legs buckled a little.

Somehow, the samurai pulled himself up behind her and hung on as Jessie wheeled the palomino around and made it run.

"We've got to warn the cowboys to turn that herd away before they catch wind of that grass and water," Ki said, feeling his heart starting to bang against his ribs.

"I know," Jessie said, "but I'd rather lose them all a million times over than to lose you."

Ki leaned his head against Jessie's back and tried to hang on. He could feel rivers of fire surging through his blood along with chills and fever. He was going to die. He was sure of it. Die just as meanly as the vulture and his own poor horse.

A terrible spasm shook his length and, unbidden, his arms and legs lost their strength and began to shake uncontrollably.

77

He could not hold on. Ki felt himself falling and he heard Jessie scream. He struck the earth and rolled over and over. When he came to a stop, he was twitching and choking.

"No!" Jessie screamed, tearing her gun from its holster, jamming it between Ki's teeth and trying to keep him from swallowing his tongue.

"Hang on!"

Ki could not hang onto anything. He had lost control of his body, something that he had never expected, never considered, and had driven himself for so many years to avoid. He had always treated his body like a temple, refusing to pollute it with alcohol, opium, or even tobacco. He'd seen so many men ruin their own bodies that he would never do such a thing. He'd seen young opium addicts who should have been virile and strong reduced to quivering shells. He'd all too many times seen other once-powerful men laid to waste by liquor.

And now, despite all he had done, he found himself being reduced to nothing more than a terrified mind inside a dying, poisoned body.

"Ki!" Jessie cried, scooping up his head and cradling it in her lap. "Oh, Ki!"

He was aware of tears drenching her face and Ki tried to tell her that the loss of his life was not worthy of great sorrow, but he could not speak. His body kept shaking uncontrollably and Ki almost wished for death.

"I've got to leave you and go for help," she said. "You'll die if I don't find some help!"

Ki didn't want her to leave him helpless and alone. If another lowly turkey buzzard saw him in this condition, it could sweep down, land on his chest and peck his eyes out and he would be powerless to resist. Ki tried to tell this to Jessie, but no words came to his mouth.

Jessie remounted Sun and whipped the gaunt animal into a hard run back toward her approaching herd. She could plainly see the dust raised by her cattle and knew that they would be less than three miles away now. And if they did manage to get the scent of water and grass, it would be nearly impossible to turn them away.

Sun ran like the wind even in his weakened condition, and when, from the distance, the cowboys saw Jessie without the samurai, they knew something was terribly wrong.

Pete and Len spurred out ahead of the herd and Jessie wasted no time in explaining that a pool of death lay just a couple of miles behind her.

"Ki may be dying," she choked. "Get the herd turned."

"What direction?"

"Northeast! Get them turned before it's too late."

Pete twisted in his saddle and swore. "Look, Miss Starbuck, that brindle is way out in front and he already senses grass and water."

"Shoot him and turn the rest back!" Jessie cried. "Tell Scotty Duggan to get his wagon out here as fast as he can. There's some quinine and other medicine in the wagon but I don't know if anything can save Ki now."

Pete Willis yanked his gun out of its holster and so did Len. They raced toward the brindle bull which was about a quarter mile ahead of the other cattle and coming like a freight train.

Jessie waited to see the two cowboys intercept the brindle. She saw them raise their guns and fire into the air, trying to dissuade the bull from its course. They might as well have been attempting to change the course of the Rio Grande River. The brindle just lowered its big head and kept shuffling forward.

"Shoot him!" Jessie cried, knowing her shouts would not be heard over the distant gunfire.

Pete grabbed his lariat and Len did the same. They both roped the big bull, dallied their lariats around their saddlehorns, and spurred off toward the northwest. Jessie saw the brindle dig in its hooves, but it was too weak to stop the horses from dragging it off the scent of water and grass.

The brindle was dragged across the path of the onrushing herd, confusing everything. For a moment,

79

the fate of the herd tottered between the disaster of stampeding toward the poison water and following their leader.

The brindle bawled in frustration and anger. A secondary leader bawled in return and then swerved off-course to follow the brindle. Others fell in, abruptly changing direction until the entire herd was moving off to the northwest. They were bawling and lowing and raising hell with the brindle as if it had been his fault that everything was in confusion.

Jessie wiped the tears from her eyes and wheeled her horse around. The herd would live for a few more days at least, even without good water. She prayed that she could say the same thing for her brave and beloved samurai.

★

Chapter 11

Scotty Duggan showed remarkable youth and agility when he jumped off the seat of his chuckwagon and ran to Ki's side.

"What is it?" Donita cried, also coming to rest beside the samurai.

"I don't know," Jessie admitted, furious at herself for being so helpless and ignorant. "Something in the water that can't be tasted or seen. Something very deadly."

The samurai had already lapsed into a coma. His pulse was racing, his body was cold, and he was knotted up at the belly as if in great pain. Even his fists were knotted and his lips were drawn back in a grimace. The barrel of Jessie's revolver was still jammed between his clenched jaws.

"We've got to try something," Jessie whispered. "Get the quinine and that bicarbonate of soda out of the medicine chest! Hurry!"

Sonny Lane hobbled down from the wagon, his ankle still giving him fits. He knelt beside Ki. "He's a goner unless we can find out what kind of medicine to give him."

Jessie's green eyes flashed. "Well if you have any ideas, let's hear them."

"The Comanche," Sonny told her. "They've been living on this land for centuries, they might have some medicine that would work."

Jessie blinked. Of course! Surely over the centuries they'd had horses, dogs, children, even some of their own people who must have drunk this poisoned water. So might not they also have medicine?

"Miss Starbuck," old Scotty Duggan protested, "you can't be takin' that advice seriously."

Jessie looked down at Ki. "Look at him," she ordered. "Neither quinine nor bicarbonate of soda will do much for whatever is poisoning him."

"But you don't know that for sure!" Scotty protested. "Maybe it will heal him."

"And if it doesn't?" Jessie shook her head. "All my life I'd never forgive myself for not doing everything humanly possible to save Ki from a horrible death."

Jessie stood up. "I've got to go find Chief Gray Wolf and ask if he or his people have a cure."

"I'm going with you," Pete Willis said.

The other cowboys all volunteered to go too but Jessie shook her head. "Pete, you and Sonny come along. The rest of you stay here. Donita, you stay right with Ki and try to make him as comfortable as you can. Scotty, go ahead and dose Ki with quinine, bicarbonate, and anything else we have that might work."

"I sure wish you'd change your mind and let your men go this time," Scotty said with an ominous shake of his head. "I don't trust them Indians."

Jessie looked down at the unconscious samurai. "We *have* to trust them," she said.

As soon as they were mounted, Jessie led off across the hills in the direction she'd last seen Gray Wolf and his Comanche. She rode hard and soon outdistanced both Sonny and Pete. An hour later, they saw a distant plume of smoke lifting up to the sky and Jessie reined her horse in.

"That'll be them," she said. "When we come in sight, just act as if we rode into a hostile Indian camp every day."

"I can already feel my scalp pricklin'," Sonny told her.

"Me too," Pete said.

"We'll be all right," Jessie assured them, sounding more confident than she really felt inside.

The Comanche were camped right out on the open flats. Gray Wolf's big tent was off to the right of camp and she could see the big Comanche warrior sitting alone in front of his tent.

A short distance away, the warriors were busily roasting a full side of one of Jessie's beeves and the tasty meat smell mingled with the stench of burning hide and hair.

"By God," Pete whispered, "they don't even skin 'em before they eat!"

"Shhh!" Jessie hissed.

They rode toward Gray Wolf who was seated cross-legged before his tent gnawing on a chunk of singed beef. Now, he pitched the beef aside and stood up to wait for Jessie and her cowboys to come up and speak.

"Chief Gray Wolf," Jessie began, "I have come for your help."

"Dismount," Gray Wolf grunted.

Jessie did as she was ordered. She could feel the eyes of the Comanche raking her with hostility. Ignoring their hot glances, Jessie gave her reins to Sonny and walked up to the chief. "It is our warrior," she said without wasting words on preliminaries, "he drank the poison water to the north."

Gray Wolf looked toward the north. "I know of that water. Samurai will die soon."

"No!" Jessie lowered her voice. "Chief Gray Wolf, your people's medicine is very strong. I believe that you

83

can help the samurai to fight off the poison he drank."

Gray Wolf folded his muscular arms. He was wearing leather moccasins and fringed leggings as well as a breechcloth and an army coat with the sleeves hacked off at the shoulders. He looked very formidable and not at all friendly.

"No medicine for whites," the chief grunted.

"But he's like you!" Jessie protested. "He's a warrior! And . . ." Jessie had not wanted to use this argument, but she could see that there was little choice, ". . . and he gave you your life."

Gray Wolf's eyes narrowed. He did not like to hear this, but he and his warriors knew that it was the truth.

Gray Wolf shook his head angrily. "No Indian medicine!"

"Let's get out of here!" Sonny hissed. "We're just wasting our time."

"No." Jessie stepped closer to the warrior. She knew men and this chief was all man. Maybe his pride was at stake here and he would change his mind if they could just sit down and talk this out in privacy.

"I want to talk with you alone," she said, glancing toward the tent. "We have much to say to each other."

For a moment, he did not seem to hear, then he turned and grabbed the filthy flap of the tent and opened it. He barked an order in his own tongue and the warriors pushed Sonny and Pete back.

"Hey!" Sonny cried. "What the hell is going on here! Jessie!"

"It's all right," she said. "Just stay back and don't interfere. I'm going to bargain with the chief—medicine for cattle."

"Well can't you do it out here where we can watch him."

"No," Jessie said, stepping into the tent and seeing that its floor was covered with buffalo robes and that there were several rifles and an army saddle piled over against one of the canvas walls.

Gray Wolf dropped the flap behind him and moved to Jessie. He reached out, grabbed her by the shoulders and sat her down hard on the buffalo robes. Then, he sat down right across from her.

Jessie swallowed dryly. She could feel her heart racing because the big Comanche was staring at her crotch and she recognized desire when she saw it.

"Chief Gray Wolf," she began, "I will give you many cattle if you make strong medicine and save my warrior."

"How many?" he asked, finally lifting his eyes to her face.

Jessie had anticipated this question and had a ready answer. "If you come to my camp and make medicine, even if it fails, I will give you ten beeves. If you save the warrior's life, I will give you fifty."

Gray Wolf's eyes widened a little because this was indeed a very generous offer. But then, his face hardened. "No," he said. "Fifty beeves and Mexican woman. I want her."

"Donita?"

Gray Wolf nodded vigorously.

Jessie's heart sank. She had not expected this demand and could see no way to satisfy it. "I cannot do that," she said. "The Mexican girl is not for trade."

The Comanche's rough features darkened with anger. "I want her!"

"No," Jessie said again. "If your medicine will save Ki, I will give you more beeves. I'll give you my horse, my guns. I will give you money. Anything, but not a life."

The muscles in Gray Wolf's cheeks corded like rope and he started to come to his feet. Jessie, knowing that she had just forfeited the samurai's life, threw herself forward and grabbed the chief before he could turn and stomp his way outside.

"A hundred cattle," she pleaded.

He froze and looked at her, his eyes hard, and then he grabbed her blouse and pulled it open, revealing her lush breasts.

Jessie shivered and stood before him not moving. "Fifty cattle if you come and fifty more if you save his life," she managed to say in a voice she did not recognize. "But if you have no medicine and are trying to trick me, then I will see that you die this day."

"We have strong medicine," he said, reaching down and unbuckling the gun on her shapely hip, then unbuttoning her pants. "Gray Wolf needs woman now."

Jessie managed to nod her head. She would have given her life to save that of the samurai and she would certainly give her body.

Gray Wolf pushed her roughly down on the buffalo rugs and tore off the rest of her clothes.

"Miss Starbuck!" Sonny cried. "Are you all right in there!"

"Yes!"

Gray Wolf grinned as he slowly undressed, and stood over her, his long, dark root extending out from his lean, muscular body. He wanted her to look at him and see what a fine specimen of manhood he really was.

Jessie looked up and wondered exactly what he would do to her. She did not have to wait long. He dropped to his knees, pulled her legs apart and studied her womanhood, admiring her light pubic hair and then stroking it, perhaps finding it much silkier than the Indian and Mexican women that he had known.

The big Indian reached out and touched her pale breasts. His eyes lost their hardness and he touched her nipples with almost childlike delight.

Jessie swallowed again and closed her eyes but he squeezed one of her nipples hard and she gasped with pain, then looked at him. It was what he wanted as he shoved his way closer between her thighs and then drew his teeth back, grabbed her by the hips, and yanked her onto his black root.

Jessie's mouth flew open as she was impaled and then she closed off a sharp cry of pain as the big warrior slowly began to move in and out on her.

"Watch!" he panted in command.

Jessie raised up on her elbows and watched as his thick rod moved in and out of her body. For the first ten or twenty thrusts, she could feel pain but then her body lubricated itself and the pain was gone. Jessie began to hear the slick slurp of their union and despite her best intentions, she could not stop her hips from moving to Gray Wolf's thrusts.

He laughed at her and Jessie flushed with anger. She tried to still her body but he dropped his finger to her womanhood and began to rub the button of her greatest passion until she was squirming with desire.

"Damn you, Gray Wolf," she whispered, staring up at his hard, brown body and the gloating look on his face.

In reply, Gray Wolf pitched forward on Jessie and began to move powerfully, his thick tool whipping her into a frenzy. Jessie's hands slipped down to his buttocks and she grabbed them and pulled frantically, wanting this to be over.

When she could barely stand it anymore, Gray Wolf suddenly stopped. Jessie's body, still pumping, tried to hold him but he pulled out of her and panted, "Now Comanche way!"

The big Indian rolled Jessie over and then lifted her hips so that she was on her knees. He moved around behind her and pushed her head down, then pulled her legs apart and drove his wet root far up into her womanhood. His hands came around and found her button of desire and he began to thrust powerfully at her as his finger brought Jessie to new, unexpected thresholds of pleasure.

"Oh . . . oh!"

"Jessie!" It was Pete Willis and he sounded frantic. "What's going on in there!"

"We're . . . oh . . . TALKING!"

A moment later, Jessie buried her forehead against the buffalo robe and stared back under her flat belly to see the Comanche's huge root stiffen and his powerful thighs grow taut as he slammed his seed deep into her body.

87

Her own desire broke like an earthen dam and she collapsed twitching and moaning into the buffalo robe.

It took them both several minutes to regain their breath and then slowly dress, not once exchanging glances.

Jessie stood up knowing that her face was flushed and she was leaking a little of his seed but not knowing what to do about it.

"You can save him?" she managed to whisper.

Gray Wolf nodded. "I have strong medicine. You know that now. I, Gray Wolf, save."

"Then let's go. But don't you dare tell them what you got in here besides my cattle."

Gray Wolf barked a laugh, pulled up his breechcloth and shoved Jessie ahead of him through the tent flap.

★

Chapter 12

Jessie sat apart from everyone and stared at Gray Wolf and the medicine man whom they had brought to help Ki. The other cowboys, sensing Jessie's dark mood of depression, had gone off a little ways and were seated or reclining on the dead grass, their expressions grim as they also watched the Comanche make their medicine.

At least, Jessie thought, the samurai was still alive. He must not have drunk as much water as his pinto horse or he would surely have expired long before she and the Comanche had returned.

For almost an hour, the two Indians had worked over a heavy black kettle filled with vile-smelling herbs and God only knew what other ingredients. Now, it appeared that the brew was almost ready.

Jessie watched as Gray Wolf, his body drenched with sweat from working over the hot fire and kettle, raised his hands to the hot, cloudless skies and began to chant some ancient song. Jessie wished to heaven that these Comanche would hurry up and simply give the unconscious samurai their concoction. If it saved Ki, everything would have been worth the price. The cattle, her bruised body, everything. But if Ki died . . . Jessie was not sure what she would do. Her impulse would be to pull her gun and kill both the Indians.

For almost five minutes, Gray Wolf and his medicine man sang, danced, and implored the sky and sprinkled medicine from little beaded leather pouches that hung from their necks. Jessie could see that her cowboys were also becoming extremely impatient. She wondered what they would think if they knew what she had sacrificed in Gray Wolf's tent in order to induce him to come here and attempt to save Ki's life.

Jessie had no regrets. Even if the samurai died, she would spend however many years she might live knowing that she had done everything possible to save her best friend.

The two Comanche suddenly stopped singing and dancing. Jessie watched as they took pinches of dust or some kind of powder from a medicine jar and held it up to the four corners of the world. Both Indians whispered fervent prayers and when the dust was evenly distributed to the four winds, they used a gourd to scoop off some of their steaming brew before they turned to the samurai.

Jessie and her cowboys tensed as Gray Wolf removed the pistol barrel from between Ki's clenched teeth and then pried open the samurai's jaw very wide before the medicine man poured the hot liquid into Ki's open mouth. Ki choked and sputtered. It was all that Jessie could do not to protest because she was afraid Ki would choke to death.

The medicine man jumped back to the steaming kettle and ladled more of his brew, then poured another full measure down Ki's throat.

Jessie moved forward but did not interfere. She knew that the samurai was a dead man if this Comanche medicine failed.

"It's got to be scalding his throat," she whispered.

Sonny Lane firmly took her arm. "I think you better let 'em pour just as much of that stinkin' stuff down his throat as they want, Miss Jessie. It's the only chance your friend has got of stickin' in this world."

"I know. I know," Jessie said. "But what if all they're doing is burning his throat?"

"They want them cattle you promised real bad," Sonny reminded her. "And though they ain't admitting it, I figure they got as much at stake in saving Ki's life as we do."

Jessie forced herself to relax. Sonny was right. A lot of cattle hung in the balance here and these Comanche were hungry. Of course, they could always try and take the herd by force, but Gray Wolf and his medicine man must have noted that the Circle Star cowboys looked tough and that stealing the herd would be very costly in terms of Comanche lives.

Twice more Gray Wolf pried open the samurai's clenched jaws so that his medicine man could pour their vile concoction down Ki's throat. Jessie could do little more than watch and fret.

When it appeared that the two Comanche weren't going to administer any more of their brew to the samurai, they again began to dance and chant. Jessie and her cowboys settled in for a long session and their eyes kept sweeping back and forth between the two Indians and the prostrate samurai.

"Maybe it's a good time for you to take a nap," Sonny told her. "You've got some pretty dark circles under your eyes. You can't do any good watching."

As much as Jessie wanted to wait, she knew that Sonny was right.

She was rundown and bone-weary from long hours in the saddle and the rough session of lovemaking she'd had with Gray Wolf.

"All right. But promise to wake me if there is any change in Ki's condition—either way."

"I promise," Sonny told her.

Jessie went over to her bedroll and pulled it under the chuckwagon so that she would be out of the sun. She spread her bedroll and fell asleep almost instantly.

"Jessie!"

She was so tired that she had not even dreamed during the hours of her sleep. When Jessie opened her eyes, it was dark and she looked up to see Sonny's face bathed in the firelight.

"He woke up," Sonny told her quite simply. "The samurai is awake and talking."

Jessie sat up so fast she banged her forehead on the underside of the chuckwagon. "Ouch!"

"Here," Sonny said, "you're still half-asleep. Let me help you out."

He pulled Jessie out from under the wagon. "How long have I been asleep!"

"About eight hours."

"And Ki just woke up?"

Sonny nodded. "Asked for you first thing."

Jessie staggered erect. Sonny took her arm and guided her around the campfire past grinning cowboys. Gray Wolf and the medicine man were seated off in the semidarkness, silent as stones.

"Ki!"

The samurai rolled over on his side and he smiled when he saw Jessie.

"Thank God you are alive."

"God maybe, the Comanche deserve some thanks too," Ki said. "I feel as if I have been to hell and back."

Jessie knelt at the samurai's side. She wanted to bawl with gratitude. Ki must have seen this because he reached up and touched her cheek. "I had visions," he said.

Jessie sniffled. Ki still looked very pale and weak, but she knew now that he would recover quite rapidly. She had seen him many times before when his strength had been almost exhausted in some battle, only to make a near miraculous recovery.

92

"I saw Hirata," Ki whispered, a smile creasing his face. "And I saw a vision of this herd reaching Kansas."

Jessie did not believe in visions, but she did not want to dampen the samurai's enthusiasm. "Did we *all* make it to Kansas?"

"Not all," Ki said, his smile fading. "There are many dangers yet ahead of us."

"I see." Jessie did not want to hear any more of this vision if it foretold that more of her cowboys might die. "Will you be strong enough to travel in the wagon tomorrow?"

Ki nodded his head.

"Good!"

Jessie came to her feet and walked over to the two Comanche. The moment she was with them, Gray Wolf stepped in very close to her. He would have reached out and touched her breasts but Jessie stepped back.

"Your medicine was strong," she told them both. "And I am of my word. In the morning, when the sun is off the earth, bring your warriors here and I will give you the beeves I have promised."

Gray Wolf dropped his hands to his side. He looked deeply into Jessie's eyes and she saw his hunger for her again was rekindled. This seemed remarkable considering how hard he and his medicine man had worked, sweated, and prayed to save Ki.

Gray Wolf said, "I would give you back ten beeves if you would walk with me under the stars."

"I . . . I can't," she said, not wanting to offend this proud Comanche chief. "But I will always remember us together."

Gray Wolf nodded solemnly. His shoulders dropped a little with disappointment, but he was a man who had known many disappointments in his life and was disciplined enough to accept this one with grace. He reached out and touched Jessie's cheek and then he turned and vanished into the night with his medicine man.

Sonny had been standing nearby. "That big chief seemed to have quite an attraction to you, Miss Jessie."

She turned. "Oh really?"

"Well . . . well I just thought that . . ."

"Let's all turn in for the night," she said. "Just two night herders and I'll take the first shift since I've had a good rest."

"I'd like to take the same," Sonny told her. "Just in case that big buck takes it into his mind that he might like more than beef."

"He won't," Jessie said. "He's a man of honor. His warriors and his people are hungry. He will take the cattle tomorrow morning and leave us alone."

Sonny nodded. "I'd still like to ride night herd with you on the first shift."

"All right," she said, relaxing. "Just as long as you keep your eyes on the herd and not on me."

Sonny laughed. "Easier said than done, Miss Starbuck. But I'll try."

Jessie went to get her horse and saddle it for the first watch. The moon had slipped behind a cloud and it was pretty dark, but the stars were gleaming, and when she passed Ki she saw that he had fallen asleep and was resting easy.

A few minutes later as Jessie mounted her horse and turned it out toward her herd, she thought about Gray Wolf and his rough lovemaking. With just a little consideration, she thought, that big Comanche Indian would be a hell of a fine lover. But then, maybe the Comanche women liked their men to take them that way.

No matter. Indian medicine had saved Ki's life and as Jessie turned Sun into the herd and gazed up at the heavens, she felt very very good about herself and the way everything had turned out.

Sonny rode up beside her and they rode stirrup to stirrup for nearly a quarter of an hour before Sonny said, "Know what?"

"What?"

"I didn't think all that Indian medicine and their singing and dancing would do a thing for Ki. I thought he was a goner."

"I thought maybe so too," Jessie admitted. "But that just goes to show you how much we don't know about the Indian and about the natural medicines they use."

Sonny frowned. "I heard the samurai say that we've got a peck more of trouble facing us before we reach the Kansas railhead."

"That's right."

"And he said that we wouldn't all get there, isn't that right?"

Jessie turned to look at the Texas cowboy. "That's right. Sorry you came?"

"No ma'am!" Sonny rode along for a few minutes. "But knowing a few of us are going to die does give a body something to ponder, doesn't it."

Jessie nodded. It sure as hell did.

★

Chapter 13

Ki was back on a horse in less than a week and just the sight of him riding out in front of their herd was enough to lift everyone's spirits. And it seemed to Jessie that as they traveled north up into the Texas Panhandle country, the land wasn't quite so tortured by lack of water. More and more often, they found springs and feed as well as good water for the cattle.

In order to keep his skills sharp and regain his conditioning, the samurai would stalk deer and antelope on foot. Down south, this game was very rare during the drought, but up here it was far more common, and the cowboys appreciated a change from the steady diet of beef that had been their main staple during the first several hundred miles of the trail drive.

"The cattle are starting to put on a little bit of flesh again," Bob Hanes said one afternoon as he rode beside

Jessie. "That brindle bull leadin' 'em looked like a hat rack he was so bony when we left. Now, he's almost starting to look like he might make someone a good steak."

Jessie laughed. "If that brindle gets this herd all the way up to Kansas again this year, I'll retire him on the ranch."

"Might be that he'd not want to come back," Hanes opined. "Not if he finds good, green grass up in Kansas."

"He'll either come back or wind up on someone's platter," Jessie said.

"Maybe I better explain that to him right now," Hanes said, touching spurs to the flanks of his horse and using that little excuse to go back to work.

Jessie rode along on the left flank of the herd, the sun hot on her back. She removed her Stetson and wiped her brow, then returned the hat to her head. It seemed to her that it might never be cool again. Every day since they had left her Circle Star Ranch, the temperature had been at least ninety-five degrees and often well over one hundred. The heat could sure sap the strength out of a person, Jessie thought as she gazed north in search of a thunderhead that might herald a welcome change in the weather.

"Miss Jessie?"

Jessie turned in her saddle to see Len Cooper come galloping up. Len was a tall, quiet young man of about nineteen. He was freckled, sandy-haired, and decidedly bucktoothed. The first time one of the cowboys had tried to nickname him "rabbit" Len had whipped the man so thoroughly that no one had dared to tease him again about his front teeth, which were almost continually exposed in a grin.

To Jessie's way of thinking, Len was an easygoing young man except when it came to being teased about his prominent front teeth, and he was a very good cowboy. In fact, Len Cooper admitted that he had learned to rope from an old vaquero, and his flourishing style with the long leather reata left no doubters.

Jessie liked the boy, but right now he appeared disturbed about something.

"Miss Starbuck," he said, "I got to talk to you. I just *got* to before something terrible happens."

Len was not the kind of boy to get excited about small things and the urgency in his voice caused Jessie to take sharp notice. "What's wrong?"

Len fell in beside Jessie. He was upset and so nervous that he fiddled with his reata for a full minute or two before he said, "It's about Miss Donita."

"What about her?"

"Well, you know how she stuck so close to the samurai when she first came?"

"Yes."

"And how he sorta got tired of it and maybe told her to back off a little?"

"I don't know anything about that," Jessie said, trying to guess where this conversation was leading. "But, yes, I've noticed that she's leaving him alone now."

"Well," Len said, "everybody has noticed."

"You'd do a lot better to keep your mind on the cattle," Jessie said, afraid that she knew where this conversation was leading.

"Yeah, yeah, I know that."

"Donita has had a very hard time of things," Jessie said. "She needs some time to sort out her thoughts. I've already made it plain that she is not to be bothered by anyone."

"Oh," Len said with a violent shake of his head. "I'd never 'bother' her, Miss Starbuck. I swear to God I wouldn't! I just admire her from afar when she crosses my vision. That's all."

"Good. Then what is the problem?"

"Well, it's Sonny Lane, ma'am."

"What?"

"Yes, ma'am! He's been pesterin' that girl some."

Jessie was not pleased by this declaration and not sure that she believed it anyway. "Be more specific."

"Well I just saw Miss Donita cryin' and when I asked her what was wrong, she looked off at Sonny and gave him the worst look you ever saw."

"I don't believe that for a minute. Sonny is a ladies' man, I know that. But he also knows that I wouldn't tolerate anyone bothering that girl. Besides, there's no opportunity out here."

"Well," Len said, shaking his head, "he's got her bothered. I ain't sayin' he's touched her or anything, but she's right bothered."

"And she said that?"

"No, miss, she did not. I could just tell from the way that she looked at Sonny that he was the cause of her tears."

Jessie sighed with exasperation. "I'll talk to her, Len. But I think you're letting your imagination get the better of you."

"No ma'am! I saw Sonny give her some wild flowers the other day when we found 'em in that grassy meadow. He picked some when nobody but me was watchin' and he walked right up to Miss Donita and gave them all to her. Every last one."

Jessie's brow furrowed. If what Len said was true, there was indeed a problem. The men knew and respected her enough not to be a bother, but Donita, being confused and emotionally as well as physically vulnerable, was entirely another matter. The Circle Star cowboys were damned decent men—but they were all strong and virile young men who had not had a chance to make love in a good long while.

"I'll talk to Donita tonight after we settle in," Jessie promised.

"I'd appreciate it if you didn't mention it was me that brought this up. I don't want to seem forward."

"Thanks," Jessie said. "You were right to bring this to my attention. If there's a problem, then we need to handle it right away before things get worse."

Len started to rein his horse away, then hesitated. "Miss Starbuck, Sonny is a good man. I don't mean to cause him any grief. It's just that he's had women troubles before."

"What do you mean?" Jessie demanded.

Len blushed. "I can't rightly say. You'd have to ask him."

"But I'm asking you." Jessie was getting angry. "Is there something else I should know about his past?"

"I'm sorry, Miss Starbuck. What I heard was just talk and I'd rather not say any more."

Before Jessie could say another word, Len tipped his Stetson and galloped way to leave her confused and troubled.

Ki did not return to camp that evening but stayed out on the prairie, perhaps many miles out in front of the herd and hopefully near grass and water that they would need for the stock tomorrow.

Jessie had fretted about Len's warning all afternoon and now, since Ki was not close to advise her, she motioned old Scotty Duggan aside after dinner. Scotty had a pronounced limp so Jessie did not go any farther than was absolutely necessary.

"I'd like to talk to you," she said when they were clearly out of earshot.

"Someone complaining about my coffee being too strong again?" he demanded.

"No."

"Then it's got to be my sourdough biscuits."

"No," Jessie said, "the biscuits are just fine. There are no complaints about your cooking."

"Then what . . ."

"It's the girl," Jessie said, cutting the old cowboy turned cook off, "I've heard that she's upset by Sonny. Is there anything to that?"

Scotty had been about to say something, but now he clamped his jaw shut and jammed his hands deep into his pockets. "Ain't none of my business," he mumbled.

"Well it is my business because Donita's welfare is my responsibility. And if Sonny or anyone else is bothering her, then I need to know about it."

"Maybe he is a little," Scotty said. "But then again, maybe she wants to be bothered."

"What is that supposed to mean?"

"I don't know. You're a woman, you tell me, Miss Starbuck. One time I catch that halfbreed girl smilin' at Sonny like she's got extra teeth for sale, the next, she's crying. I don't know nothin' about it is what I'm tellin' you."

Jessie sighed. "Is he bothering her?"

"Not that I can see. Oh, he looks at her a lot, but so do the others. Hell, *I* even look."

"I see." Jessie toed the hard, dry earth. "I guess I had better talk to the cowboys tomorrow about that girl. She could cause a lot of trouble."

"Already is, the way I figure it. Ain't much help to me anymore."

"Thanks," Jessie said, turning to leave.

"A girl like that is no good on a trail drive," Scotty said. "She'll sashay around and cause us more grief than the Indians."

"Well we can't just abandon her out here, now can we," Jessie demanded with more than a hint of exasperation. "We've got to take her to a city or at least a decent-sized town and find someone responsible to take care of her."

Scotty Duggan snorted. "Every last cowboy on this drive would like to be that someone, Miss Starbuck. That's a handsome breed."

"She's not a 'breed,' " Jessie snapped. "She's a young woman who's been through a terrible ordeal and who has shown remarkable courage."

"Yep," Scotty said, "but she's gonna be a heap of trouble for us if she stays."

Jessie stomped on back to the camp. She knew that Scotty was right and she knew that she had to have a hard talk with the men before there were any more rivalries created over the girl. One thing sure, Jessie had a sense that Donita wasn't going to cooperate and make things any easier.

101

★

Chapter 14

Jessie waited until her cowboys were all mounted, and then she motioned them to follow her out around the herd and away from camp so that Donita would not be angered or hurt by what she had to say.

"Boys," Jessie said when she pulled her horse in, "I've heard that we have some problems with Miss Donita."

The cowboys suddenly took a big interest in their hands, the manes of their horses, their ropes, anything to avoid meeting Jessie's eyes. If she had had any doubts there was a problem with the girl, those doubts were now dispelled. There was a problem and she should have sensed it herself.

"From now on, I want to make sure that we all understand each other. Miss Donita is to be left strictly alone. She has gone through hell as a Comanchero captive and I will attempt to find her a proper and responsible place to live when we reach the Kansas railheads. Until then,

I want no man to talk to her unless she speaks to him first, and then only answer her questions, politely, but concisely."

"Con-what?" a cowboy asked.

"Concisely," Jessie repeated. "That means in as few words as possible."

Jessie looked right in Sonny's eyes. "If any man here can't abide by those rules, speak up right now."

No one said a word except Sonny. "And what if the girl doesn't want to be farmed out to some family in Kansas?"

"Then," Jessie said, "I'll just have to try and think up something better. But that's my intention at this point and I won't have anyone playing romantic games with Donita. She's probably lonely and confused. She needs a little time away from men, not with them, but circumstances being what they are, we'll do the best we can. Any other questions?"

Sonny was angry. She could see that his face was red and he kept glancing over at Len, who wouldn't match his eye. Finally, Sonny snapped, "I'd like to know what brought this all about."

"Just an observation on my part," Jessie lied.

"No offense, Miss Starbuck," Sonny grated, "but that 'girl' as you call her, is a grown woman and she ought to be able to make her own mind up who she does or does not want to talk to. Furthermore, I'd be plenty willing to bet that the samurai sure didn't treat her like a girl."

"That's enough of that talk!" Jessie said angrily. "Sonny, you either ride by my rules, or I'll pay you off and you can ride out of here now."

Sonny's face went from red to pale white. "You're maybe forgetting I've been damn loyal to you, Miss Starbuck. And this is no way to repay me."

If they had not been hundreds of miles from civilization, Jessie would have fired Sonny Lane on the spot. But he was a good cowboy, a fine shot, and a brave man—all qualities that she very much needed on this long cattle drive north. Firing Sonny now would put a hardship on all the cowboys.

"You'll be repaid in Kansas. Probably at Abilene," Jessie said. "And until then, you'll do as I say or draw your gear and move out."

"It ain't right and I don't know what Len told you, but he lied!"

"One more word and you're fired, Sonny." Jessie's voice was flat and hard. "You've been a good man and I don't want to let you go, but I won't have feuding on this cattle drive. We've troubles enough to face without creating more of our own."

Sonny shot a murderous glance at Len and then he viciously yanked his mount around and spurred away. Jessie watched him for several minutes, then she said, "All right, men. Let's get these cattle moving north."

For the next two days, everything went fine. They found water and Ki shot a nice buck, so they had roast venison. But on the third afternoon, when Jessie was riding about a mile out ahead of the herd with Ki, Bob Hanes came whipping his horse up to them.

"Ki, Miss Jessie, you better come along quick. We got trouble!"

"What is it!"

"It's Sonny. He boiled over and him and Len Cooper were beatin' each other's brains out when I saw them last. I think Sonny will stomp Len to death if he gets the better of it."

Jessie shot Ki a startled glance and they both raced back toward the herd. When they arrived at the scene of the fight, Sonny was on top of Len and beating his face with his bloody fists.

"Stop it!" Jessie cried.

But Sonny was insane. Donita was standing close by and she was crying softly. Jessie yanked her sixgun, aimed it over Sonny's head and unleashed a shot that could not have missed the big cowboy's skull by more than two inches.

Sonny's bloody hand stabbed for his sixgun but when he saw it was Jessie, he froze.

"Get off of your horse," Jessie ordered.

Ki dismounted and went to Len, who was conscious, but whose face was battered and a frightful mess.

"Maybe you should try me," Ki said.

"Maybe," Sonny panted, his broad chest heaving, "maybe I'll do that sometime."

"Not on my payroll you won't," Jessie swore. "You're fired."

Sonny spun around to face her. "Ain't you even going to ask me what happened!"

For a moment, Jessie almost did. "No," she said finally. "You're trouble. And I won't have a man who goes crazy in a fight and beats another one of the crew half to death."

Jessie dismounted and went over to the chuckwagon. "Scotty, give me my strongbox."

Scotty got it in a hurry. Jessie kept a key on a chain around her neck and she unlocked the box. "I owe you about sixty dollars," she said, counting out the money. "And that's on the generous side. Here."

Sonny, his own face plenty marked up, stomped over to Jessie and took the money. "This ain't right," he growled. "That girl has been leading me on. No man could have stayed away any longer than I did."

"Get on your horse and ride," Ki said.

Sonny turned on Ki. "I never liked the idea of working for a woman who kowtowed to a Oriental. You must have something pretty damn big between your legs to get her to . . ."

Whatever else Sonny was going to say was lost as Ki's hand chopped through the air and caught him at the base of the neck. Sonny's eyes rolled up in his head and he collapsed in a pile.

Jessie called for a basin of water and some rags so that she could clean up poor Len.

"Let me do it," Donita offered, her eyes glistening with tears.

"I think you've done enough already," Jessie said, wiping Len's face clean. "Scotty, Pete, let's keep him in the chuckwagon for a couple of days. He's pretty bad off."

The two men helped carry Len to the chuckwagon and when he was loaded, Jessie said, "Let's get this herd moving."

"Are you going to just leave him here like that!" Donita cried.

"He'll come around soon enough," Ki assured her.

"But what if the Indians come around first!"

Ki didn't care. "He's a survivor," Ki said. "He'll be all right."

"But you don't know that!"

"Let him go," Ki said.

"He wants to marry me!" Donita cried. "He said he'd marry me when we came to the first town."

Jessie stepped closer. "I don't think you could trust the man, Donita. He was going to use you. Take advantage of your . . . troubles."

"You're just saying that because he started liking me better than you!"

Jessie sighed. "I don't think so. Anyway, once I get you to Abilene or someplace safe, you can go off on your own if you want. If Sonny was telling the truth, he'll find you. But I ordered him and the others to let you be and he chose to ignore my orders. I can't have that."

Donita cupped her face in her hands and wept. Ki looked away, but Scotty put his arms around her waist and, in a voice surprising for its gentleness, he said, "Come along Miss Donita. He wasn't the man for you anyway. The kid he whipped is a whole lot finer fella."

Jessie never looked back and neither did the rest of the crew as they got the herd moving. They left the unconscious cowboy his gun, rifle, a sack of provisions, and his horse. Ki told them that Sonny would regain consciousness within a few hours, and everyone figured he'd strike out directly east toward the nearest town along the Red River.

"I have a confession to make," Jessie said to Ki when they were out in front and alone again. "I was strongly attracted to that man. I . . . well, I had to be careful not to be around him too much for fear that it would show."

"I could tell," Ki said. "And if he could fool someone like you, it's easy to see how he could also fool a girl like Donita."

"Well," Jessie said. "At least he didn't hurt her. Poor Len is going to be laid up for several days. His eyes are both swollen nearly shut."

Ki had noticed. He had also decided that, since he liked the young cowboy and it had taken courage to oppose an older, more experienced man in a bad fight, that he would teach Len a few samurai blows.

"Ki?"

"Yes?"

"I wish that we were pulling into Abilene right now."

"So do I," Ki told her, thinking about his near-death visions, "but we've still got a long, long ways to go."

★

Chapter 15

"The Canadian River," Jessie said late one afternoon as she stood up in her stirrups and gazed down at the silver thread of water. "I was wondering if we'd ever get this far."

"I also had my doubts," Ki admitted. "I was never that worried about the Comanche, or even the Comancheros, but I was afraid that the herd might starve to death before we could find good feed."

"Well," Jessie said, "there's plenty down there just waiting for us but we'd better make sure that there's no quicksand."

Jessie and Ki rode down and then separated, each riding a half mile up and down the river. Neither found any quicksand or hidden danger. When they came together again, Jessie reined her horse about and motioned for her cowboys to drive the herd on down and to let them run if they were of a mind.

The old one-eyed brindle bull was of a mind to run

and he shot out in the lead, bawling and tossing his great horns much like a man might wave his arms in excitement.

The Circle Star cowboys just stood back and let the herd charge down the hillside toward the river. A few minutes later, the cattle were lined for a good half mile up and down the banks of the Canadian, slaking their thirsts and lowing with pleasure.

"We'll stay here a couple of days and let them rest and gather their strength for the rest of the drive," Jessie told the samurai.

"I'm sure that you'll have no complaints about that," Ki said, watching as Scotty Duggan drove their chuckwagon over to some trees and prepared to set up camp.

"Think you can find us some more venison?"

Ki nodded. "Maybe even some antelope for steaks."

"That would be a treat," Jessie said.

Ki and Jessie, along with the others, rode upriver of the cattle and dismounted. They knelt beside the river and splashed cool water on their faces and scrubbed the backs of their necks. Their horses drank as if they had a fever and no one said a word for a good long time.

"I sure wish we could run this river down to the ranch," Pete Willis finally said.

Someone snickered and, as she had a thousand times so far, Jessie glanced up at the cloudless blue skies wondering if it would ever rain in Texas again. Of course, it most certainly would, but she hoped it would be pretty soon. Her foreman, Ed Wright, would also be looking to the skies and praying for rain which would soak into the cracked, parched earth and bring forth the grass their cattle so desperately needed.

Later that afternoon when the sun was starting to lose its searing intensity, Jessie saw Ki take his bow and quiver of arrows before heading off on foot up the river.

"I'll never understand," Len Cooper said, "why any man would rather walk than ride a good horse."

Jessie smiled at the remark. Len had pretty much recovered from his savage beating. No one had seen or heard Sonny Lane since his firing and Donita appeared to have gotten over her infatuation with the handsome young cowboy.

"A man on a horse," Pete Willis said, "sure couldn't stalk an antelope and put an arrow through its gizzard."

"Why'd he want to shoot an arrow anyway, if he had a rifle?" Len asked.

"It's just his way," Jessie said.

Len nodded and said, looking at Donita. "No one has to tell me that Ki is a hell of a man. I just think he'd be even more dangerous with a rifle and a pistol."

"No he wouldn't," Donita said a bit sharply. "He shouldn't change anything."

Len blushed. Flustered by the girl's sharp defense of the samurai, he mumbled something about not really meaning what he'd said and then he walked off to examine his horse.

Jessie went over to the girl. Ever since Jessie had fired Sonny Lane, Donita had treated her coolly. Jessie took the girl aside so that they could speak in private.

"Len is smitten with you, Donita. And I think you've hurt his feelings."

"Feelings mend," Donita snapped. "Either that, or they just go away."

"Not always," Jessie argued patiently. "There are times when they just fester inside. Maybe the fact that Ki feels so obligated to the protection of me and this herd has hurt you very much."

Donita's eyes flashed. "Why should it? If Ki chooses to worship you, then . . ."

"Stop it!" Jessie said sharply. "Ki doesn't 'worship' me or anyone else. He is simply a man who feels it is his duty to protect my interests."

"But you don't even love him!"

"Of course I do," Jessie said. "I just don't *make* love to him. That's a very important distinction you need to understand."

"But I don't understand," Donita cried. "And if I can't

have him and you don't want him as a man, then none of us are going to be happy."

Jessie sighed. "I know it's hard to understand," she said, "but Ki is very different. The way it is between us is as much because of his preference as my own."

Donita shook her head in disbelief. "You mean . . . you mean he doesn't want to make love to someone as beautiful as you?"

"That's right."

Donita threw up her hands in exasperation. "I can't believe that. Especially since you let Gray Wolf do it to you in his tent."

The girl was looking right into Jessie's eyes and she would have detected the least hint of a lie.

"Did Sonny tell you I made love to Gray Wolf?"

Donita nodded. "He said you wouldn't let one of your men touch you, but you'd rut with an Indian."

"I didn't have any choice," Jessie said. "It was that, or Gray Wolf wouldn't have used his medicine to save Ki's life."

Donita stared at her hard before she nodded her head and then tears welled up in her eyes. "I should have known that was the reason. But Sonny told me you just wanted that big Comanche. I'm sorry."

The girl threw herself into Jessie's arms and cried. Jessie let her get it all out. Donita was five or six years younger than herself but she was as naive as a little child. The poor thing had been raped and beaten and probably had never known real love from a man or possibly even a father. She'd fallen for Ki, who could not give his heart to her, then she'd fallen for Sonny Lane who had no heart to give. It was little wonder that she was so confused and upset.

"Listen to me," Jessie said softly as she held the quaking girl. "I've been putting some thought to your future. I want you to return with us to Circle Star and live at the ranch."

Donita looked up and sniffled. "I thought you wanted to get rid of me in Abilene."

"I want to do what is best for you. And what is best is to stay with us for a few years. Perhaps you'll marry one of my cowboys and I'll even help you both to get a small start. If it ever rains again down in Southwestern Texas, it's the finest cattle country you've ever seen."

"I don't trust men anymore. I think all they want from us is to get between our legs and rut like animals."

"And there are other men who also are kind and tender," Jessie said. "You just have to learn to separate them from the rest. Sometimes, it's very difficult. Sometimes the best men are not necessarily the handsomest. In fact, that's most often the case."

"You mean that I should fall in love next time with an ugly man?" Donita asked, her voice resigned.

"Of course not!" Jessie said with a laugh. "But you do need to look a little deeper into their hearts."

Donita frowned and wiped the tears from her cheeks. "Do you think that Len Cooper is a good man?"

"Yes," Jessie said. "He just needs a few more years of seasoning to make a very good man."

"He's very brave. You should have seen the fight he gave Sonny," Donita said. "He would have whipped him if Sonny hadn't kicked him in the balls."

Jessie suppressed the urge to tell this girl that nice women did not use that term.

"And I think that Len is crazy about me."

"I think he is too," Jessie said. "But you must promise to stay away from him or you'll cause problems, not only for yourself, but for Len as well. You're a pretty girl, Donita. Pretty girls on a trail drive are bound to cause problems."

"Yes," Donita said, "I can see that now."

"Let's get some clean clothes and walk around that bend downriver and bathe before it gets dark," Jessie said.

Donita nodded quickly. She squeezed Jessie's hand and whispered, "Thanks for wanting me to live with you. But I need to think about it a while, okay?"

"Sure," Jessie said. "You're a grown woman now, you

can do whatever you want to do."

It was nearing dusk when Jessie and Donita undressed beside the river in a willow thicket, then waded out into the lazy current to scrub themselves clean with fine sand.

"Another beautiful sunset," Jessie said.

Donita nodded and smiled. She was about to say something when they both heard the brush behind them snap, and then a voice boomed.

"Well damned if maybe we haven't died and gone to heaven, Jeb! Them two naked women are as pretty as angels!"

Jessie and Donita both whirled to see three mounted horsemen. They were big, hairy men dressed in buffalo coats despite the heat. They cradled buffalo rifles across the forks of their saddles and all of them were grinning.

"Go away!" Jessie shouted, as she and Donita squatted down in the water.

"Go away," the one on the the sorrel horse said. "Hell, ladies, we could use a bath ourselves! I think we'll just tie up our horses and come in to join you!"

"No!" Jessie warned. "I've got a camp full of cowboys just upriver and if you don't ride out of here right now, I'll call them and they'll make you wish you'd behaved."

All three of the buffalo hunters, bone pickers, or whatever they were turned to gaze upriver. Unfortunately, the bend was so large that it hid Jessie's camp as well as her cattle.

The man on the sorrel shook his head and dismounted. "Women," he said with a mean grin, "we are going to have our pleasure with you so you might as well enjoy it."

The three horsemen were staring so hard that they did not see Jessie's clothes and her sixgun lying in the willows. If she could reach her gun, she would have a chance.

Jessie didn't look sideways at Donita as she hissed, "Run and get help!"

113

"But . . ."

"Run!"

Donita took off running in the shallow water. She couldn't run very fast but she sure gained the buffalo men's attention. Two of them whipped their horses upriver to cut off Donita's escape and, in the confusion, Jessie began to lunge toward her clothes and her Colt.

The man who'd dismounted first finally understood what Jessie was up to and, with a roar, he threw himself forward to cut Jessie off.

Jessie lost her footing and fell at the riverbank. She scrambled, eyes fixed on her Colt.

"Oh no you don't!" the man laughed.

Jessie's fingers were just inches from her sixgun when the big man doubled up his fist and smashed her across the side of the head.

She moaned. Her fingers spasmed and clawed at the mud and then the man grabbed her by the hair and rolled her over.

"Even covered with mud you look good to me," he rumbled as he reached to unbutton his belt.

"Jeb!"

The bearded man looked up and saw his two friends whipping their horses back down the river.

"You let her get away!"

"There's a whole damn trail drive up just beyond the bend! They'll be coming after us!"

Jeb swore and rebuckled his belt. He looked down at Jessie's beautiful butt and he could feel his manhood stiffen with desire.

"We're taking her with us," he announced, grabbing Jessie and dragging her to his horse.

"But Jeb! She'll slow us down too much."

"We'll lose 'em," the leader roared. "They ain't nothin' but a bunch of goddamn Texas cowboys!"

"We can run along the water until we come to that slough and then keep to it up into the oaks. They won't find us. Not very easy anyway."

"Yeah, and we can have our sport for a while. That's

all I want. Just a couple of hours."

The two men licked their lips as they stared at Jessie's voluptuous body that lay across Jeb's saddle.

"Yeah," the tall, hatchet-faced one said hoarsely. "We can always dump her if they get too damn close for comfort."

"But not before we've had our fill," the third man, a short, powerful one said.

Jeb laughed. "Just as long as you boys know enough to stand in line."

Jessie, half-dazed, heard all this but could not put the words together so that they had meaning. All she could feel was pain and when the horse under her began to run, Jessie tried to throw herself free.

"Hold still, woman!" Jeb hollered.

But Jessie fought all the harder. "Damn you, I'm Jessica Starbuck and I'll see you hang for this!"

"Starbuck? Well I heard of you, woman. Out here, though, your money don't mean spit!"

He spanked her butt hard and Jessie, instead of crying out with pain, sank her teeth into his thigh.

"Owwh!" he howled, balling up his fist and sledging it down against the side of her head. This time, Jessie felt nothing as she plunged into a world of darkness.

★
Chapter 16

A moment after Ki unleashed his arrow and the antelope jumped high into the air and then collapsed in death, he heard distant gunfire. The samurai paused and then he heard no more so he went to the antelope. In a few moments, he expertly gutted the antelope and threw it across his shoulders. With the bow still clenched in his bloody fist, he started back toward the Circle Star camp.

It wasn't until he rounded a bend and a jutting wall of sandstone that he could see the cattle and then the chuckwagon. Two steps later, he dropped the antelope beside the Canadian and began to sprint toward the camp because it was clear that something was very wrong. Cowboys were milling about Donita who was bent over trying to get her breath. The scene was all the more graphic because the halfbreed girl was stark naked.

Ki shot across the ground like the antelope he'd just slain. When he reached the knot of people, it was to hear

Donita raise her head and, taking in deep gulps of air, tell the shocked Circle Star trail crew that Miss Starbuck had been kidnapped and maybe even murdered.

Ki did not wait for anything more. Even as the other cowboys were grabbing their saddles and racing for their horses, the samurai was sprinting downriver and around the bend. When he came to the place where Jessie's clothes were still neatly piled, Ki skidded to a halt, studied the sign and knew at once that three men on horseback had taken Jessie away.

Ki spent a few precious moments studying the hoofprints, committing them to memory. He looked downriver and knew that the three men would be trying to throw off all pursuit by keeping their horses in the river.

"Hey!" Pete Willis shouted, as he and the other cowboys came galloping around the bend. "Which way did they go!"

When the riders hauled their horses up in a circle around Ki, he said, "There are only three of them and that's all the men I intend to take with me."

"Now just a damned minute!" one of the cowboys protested. "I know that Jessie would have wanted you to be in charge, but it makes no sense to only take three men. You don't know for sure what you might be up against out there."

"That's right," Ki said. "But what I don't need is a bunch of revenge-seeking cowboys."

Ki turned. "Len, you, Pete, and Bob come with me. The rest stay and guard the herd."

"The hell with that!" another cowboy swore in angry protest. "I want to go after Miss Starbuck!"

In reply, Ki unceremoniously yanked the man from his saddle and mounted his horse.

"This whole thing might be a ruse just to steal the herd," Ki said. "We don't know yet how many men were involved."

"Miss Donita said there were only three."

"There might be more close by in the hills watching us right now," Ki said. "And I'm sure they'd like nothing

117

better than for us to leave the herd without much protection."

Ki looked each man in the eye saying, "Anybody else want to argue?"

No one else offered a second protest. Ki reined his horse downriver in the fading light. The three men he had chosen followed while the other cowboys, probably disappointed in not sharing in a more exciting venture, turned their horses around and rode back to the big herd of Texas longhorns.

The three men he'd chosen were brave and accomplished horsemen, though none of them except Pete Willis could be considered expert with a gun or rifle.

Ki did not think that would matter. He hoped to overtake Jessie's abductors before sunrise and kill or capture them.

"It's going to be hard seeing their tracks when they climb out of this river," Pete said, bent low over his saddlehorn and peering for marks along the bank.

Ki said nothing. The sun went down and the moon was not strong but Ki did not waste time fretting over what would not be. He just kept riding and when they came upon the first slough, he used sign language to indicate to the other men that they were to ride slowly on while he drove his horse up through the marsh and looked for fresh exit signs of the three horsemen.

Ki's horse stepped in a hole and floundered badly. The samurai slipped off the animal and, clutching his bow, managed to pull his horse over to the bank. The animal was panicked and it had a bad few moments as it floundered a second time in soft, bottomless mud. It was all that Ki could do just to pull the animal up on solid footing and tie it to a willow branch.

Ki nocked an arrow and moved through tall tule grass up the slough. He still had not seen any indication that the men he sought had come this way but he could see that this would be an excellent place for an ambush and he wasn't taking any chances.

The samurai stepped on something that slithered away

118

in the darkness, then splashed in the water. Overhead, the first stars began to appear and several night birds called across the still, stagnant water which was bathed in pale silver. A snake swam across the water, undulating back and forth and sending ripples to the bank.

Ki halted and listened hard. He listened for several moments before he pushed ahead very cautiously. Donita had said something about these men being dressed in buffalo robes. That would mean that they were hunters and, therefore, marksmen to be reckoned with.

Ki was about to move forward again when a mud hen squawked suddenly and took to flight. The samurai raised his bow in a quick, fluid motion. A huge explosion along with a great billow of smoke blanketed the slough as Ki dropped to one knee, saw a dark shadow charging him, and calmly pulled back his bowstring and fired.

His arrow traveled less than twenty feet and Ki heard it thud meanly into flesh. The shadow that was racing at him crashed into the tall grass and Ki heard the man grunting and making strangling sounds as he was locked in the throes of death.

Ki tried to ignore the searing pain he felt in his side. He nocked another arrow and waited, hearing only the shouts of the cowboys and the splashing noise their horses made as they charged blindly into the slough.

Suddenly, Ki saw another dark shadow and then the great flash of his rifle. He heard a cry and unleashed his arrow. The enemy disappeared.

Everything was confusion and chaos. Ki heard Len shout his name and the samurai turned and raced back toward the river. A few minutes later, he saw the tall, lanky form of Len and the shorter one of Pete Willis as they struggled to pull Bob Hanes from the water.

Ki jumped back into the slough and helped. Bob wasn't moving and when they finally hauled him up on the bank, he wasn't breathing, either.

"One of those dirty sonofabitches shot him off his horse!" Willis sobbed. "I'll kill him for this!"

The man looked to be half hysterical and Ki grabbed

119

him by the collar. "Pete," he ordered, "you better stay here with Bob. At first light, take him back to camp."

"But then it'd be only you and Len against the three of them!" Pete cried.

"Against two," Ki corrected. "I think I killed one just before they opened up on you."

"Goddamn 'em! I want to kill one too!"

Ki shook his head. Pete Willis and Bob Hanes had been best friends. Pete was too emotional now to go after the likes of the men who'd taken Jessie. In his drive to exact vengeance, he'd most likely get himself killed and maybe Ki and Len too.

"Do what I say," Ki commanded. "I promise you, we'll not only kill them, but we'll also bring Jessie back safe if she hasn't already been killed."

"You swear it!"

Ki nodded. "You know that I'll give my life to save Jessie's."

"So will I," Len whispered.

"All right then," Pete choked. "But we're counting on you."

"Get your horse and let's lead them up the bank," Ki said to the young man. "Just stay behind me and don't make any more noise than you have to."

"You don't have to tell me that," Len said grimly. "I can see what kind of men we're up against and I sure as hell ain't going to give them any help in killing us."

Ki liked that attitude. It was far healthier than Pete's vengeful one and far more likely to help them save Jessie's life as well as their own. These weren't city men, they were tough, ruthless, and deadly. The fact that Bob Hanes had a bullet hole dead-center in his chest big enough to put a man's fist through was plenty proof of that.

Most of the remainder of that long, difficult night was spent advancing up the slough to its dead end.

"Three horses," Ki said, kneeling in the soft mud and tracing the hoofprints with his fingertips.

"I thought that you said you got one."

"I think I did," Ki said. "But I might not have killed

him outright. Those thick buffalo hide coats aren't easy to penetrate. I might have just nicked him."

"I hope you did more than that," Len said.

"Why, are you afraid?"

Len nodded. "Damn right I am! But I wouldn't fade out on you, Ki. I'd rather get shot than live the rest of my life knowing I was a coward."

"You're no coward," Ki said, mounting his horse. "But neither are the men who have Jessie."

"Where do you think they're heading?" Len asked, staring out into the darkness.

"I don't know," Ki said, "but starting right now, we're going to find out."

Len scraped the mud off that had packed in under his high boot heels before he mounted. "I have to tell you that I'm not as good a shot as Sonny or Pete Willis."

"I know that."

"Then why didn't you send me back with Bob's body instead of Pete?"

"Because," Ki said, "you've got the makings of a warrior."

"What?"

"Never mind," Ki said. "Let's just see if we can make up a little ground on them before sunrise."

Len followed Ki away into the darkness and although they both wanted desperately to gallop their horses, they could not because they needed to stop quite often and dismount in order to follow the tracks.

"At this rate," Len complained bitterly, "they'll be halfway to hell with Miss Starbuck come daylight."

Ki said nothing. It was true that they were falling farther and farther behind, but it sure didn't make sense to lose their quarry's tracks and then have to waste precious time doubling back and going over the same ground tomorrow morning.

"We'll catch them," Ki promised. "I just hope that it's before they join up with anyone else."

Len looked sharply at him. "Like more Comancheros or Indians?"

"Yep."

Len shook his head. "Up until now, that hadn't even entered my mind."

"It should have," Ki said. "The way you stay alive in this kind of deadly game is to think out all possibilities. All the things that can go wrong and try and prepare yourself for when they happen."

"I just want to kill them," Len said. "Kill them like they killed Bob and then get Miss Starbuck and get the hell back to the herd."

"You ever kill a man before?"

"No," Len said after several seconds. "And I never thought I'd have to."

"See what I mean," Ki said. "Now you're faced with a real possibility that you just might have to take human life. If I were you, I'd think it out real carefully so that, when that moment of decision comes, you don't hesitate."

"I won't hesitate," Len promised. "I seen what their buffalo rifle did to Bob's chest and I sure don't want it to do the same to mine. I'll kill them the minute I get them in my sights."

Ki nodded and looked away. He was relieved and encouraged at these words, because the men they were now hunting would not hesitate to kill either.

★

Chapter 17

Jessie landed on her bare back and felt her breath explode from her lungs. She heard cursing and looked up to see two of the big men who'd abducted her lifting their companion from his saddle and easing him to the ground beside her.

"Jezus kee-riest!" the man who'd knocked her unconscious shouted. "We got to get that arrow out of his belly!"

Jessie kept her eyes lidded almost shut. She was still naked and the sun was rising off the eastern horizon, flooding this hard country with glare. She listened as the wounded man moaned and cursed and whimpered.

"Get it out!" he begged. "It's tearin' my insides up. You got to get it out!"

The two men pulled his buffalo coat open and stared at the arrow embedded in dark, puckered flesh. It looked deep and stuck solid.

"Jeb, he ain't by-gawd gonna make it with that kind of gut-shot wound."

Jeb's lips pulled back from his teeth and he snarled, then backhanded the man, breaking his lips.

"Shut up! He's our little brother, ain't he! You gonna tell Ma that we just left him to die like this without even trying to save his hide!"

The second man shook his head like a dumb animal. He wiped his bloody lips with the hair on his sleeve and said, "But what the hell we gonna do? You already pulled and it won't come!"

At just that instant Jeb saw Jessie looking at them through slitted eyelids. "Hey!" he yelled, grabbing Jessie by the hair. "You ever cut an arrow out of a man been gut-shot!"

"No," Jessie said, trying to tear the man's fist from her hair. "And let go of me!"

Jeb drew a huge bowie knife from his belt and raised it over Jessie. "Woman," he hissed, "I ain't got no touch for this sort of thing so unless you be wantin' me to carve them big titties of yours clean off, you'd best get that arrow outa our brother!"

Looking up into the man's bloodshot eyes, Jessie knew that he was dead serious and that, if she refused, she'd be left drowning in her own gore.

"All right," she said, nodding her head vigorously. "But I'm no doctor. Most likely, he'll die and it won't be my fault."

"Get it out!" the wounded man begged. "Goddammit, quit stallin', Jeb!"

Jeb looked into Jessie's eyes. "Woman, you'd best save our brother. It's the only hope you got of savin' yourself."

Jessie nodded. "I'll do what I can."

She took the big knife and it was much too heavy for this kind of work but it was all Jessie had and she did not complain.

"Pull his bloody shirt back and wash around the shaft

of that arrow so that I can see where I'm cutting," she told them.

"Get your canteen and do what she says, Henry," Jeb barked.

Henry jumped to his brother's orders. A few minutes later, he returned with a canteen and quickly splashed water on the wounded man's belly causing him to howl.

"Shut up, damn you Rafe! It was just water."

Rafe whimpered and threw his eyes around crazily. "I'm too young to die, Jeb. I'm younger than either you or Henry. Why was it *me* that got shot with a damned arrow!"

"Hell if I know. Life is a sonofabitch and you just drew the short stick last night. Now be still."

Rafe raised his head to see Jessie sit up with the knife poised over his belly and the shaft of Ki's arrow protruding from his gut. Under normal circumstances, he would have been wild with lust to see Jessie's body, but now, he just pleaded, "Be good to me, woman. Don't cut me too deep so's I bleed to death. Please don't!"

Big Jeb reached out and grabbed his youngest brother by the hair and slammed his head down against the hard earth. "Don't beg her! You never beg a woman except for one thing and that ain't what she's givin' you now. Understand me!"

Rafe, his eyes glazed with pain, managed to gather enough of his wits to nod his head. He closed his eyes and whimpered, his stomach muscles knotted as hard as a board.

"He needs to relax," Jessie said. "I can't possibly get that arrow out of him if he's all tensed up."

"We got enough whiskey to get him drunk," Henry offered, starting to come to his feet and go to his saddlebags.

"No!" Jeb said, freezing his brother. "We ain't got time to get him drunk. Them Texans will be huntin' up our trail. Could be a couple of them know a little trackin'."

"But it'll hurt something awful!"

Jeb's lips twisted with contempt. "We're Culberts, damn you! We been hurtin' from the minute we was born. Now let's get this over with so we know if he's gonna live or die!"

Jessie tested the knife with her forefinger and raised a thin line of blood. The knife, as she would have expected, was razor sharp. "Hold him down so he can't move."

Jessie bent over the man, highly aware that her large breasts were as much the object of Jeb and Henry's attention as was the arrow sticking out of Rafe's belly. She placed the tip of the knife against Rafe's flesh and then she drew it hard against the skin.

Rafe began to buck and holler. "Owww! Oh, gawd, ohhh!"

Rafe's screams were cut short by the thud of Jeb's fist against his brother's jaw. Jessie yanked the bowie knife back and stared as Rafe went limp. It was very obvious that big Jeb silenced every argument with his knuckles. Effective, but not very civilized, she thought, again placing the knife's blade against Rafe's belly and making an inch-deep incision around the shaft of the arrow.

Blood leaked steadily and when Jessie put her finger into the incision, she could feel the shaft which had penetrated the abdominal cavity.

"I'll have to cut a little deeper through the muscles of the abdominal wall," she said, feeling sweat bead on her forehead.

Jessie closed her eyes for a moment so that she could better concentrate on the wound. She felt down along the slick wooden shaft of the arrow until the tips of her long, slender forefingers touched the arrowhead. Rafe's body convulsed as she probed even deeper, hoping to slip her fingernails around the arrowhead and pull it out.

"You got your hand halfway into him!" Henry cried. "Just pull it out."

Jessie's eyes popped open. "I can't 'just pull it out,' " she said. "It's one of Ki's 'chewer' arrowheads."

"What the hell is that!"

Jessie told the two brothers and Jeb cursed her in a fury. Jessie was sure that the older brother would have killed her right there and then if she hadn't been Rafe's only hope.

"I'm going to try and twist it back out," Jessie decided aloud, knowing that, if she attempted to simply pull the corkscrew blade straight back, it would tear Rafe wide open.

"Oh, jezus," Henry whispered as Jessie began to unscrew the wicked arrowhead back out of Rafe's belly, "I fell like I'm going to get sick!"

"Gawddamn you!" Henry bellowed. "You'd best not do that!"

Jessie watched as the arrow's bloody shaft slowly retracted from the man's belly. When she saw stomach lining appear, she quickly placed her hand over the wound so that the brothers could not see it and then finished removing the shaft.

"This is 'chewer'," she said, holding it up for their inspection.

Even rough, vicious men like these paled a little as they studied the sinister arrowhead.

"We better get him on his horse and git," Jeb said after a minute.

"No," Jessie said. "If we don't at least wait an hour or two for the blood to clot, your brother will bleed to death for sure."

Jeb's eyes narrowed. "An hour or two?"

Jessie nodded. "And I'm going to have to keep my finger on this wound every minute or it will open."

Jeb's face grew dark with anger. "You're just buying time for your friends," he growled.

"No," Jessie said. "I'm telling you the truth. Move your brother before the clotting is set, and he's the same as dead."

Jeb turned away quickly. Jessie had no idea if he would buy her argument, but she hoped so. Ki was coming. She knew that and when he overtook these men, he would find a way to kill them both. As for Rafe, well,

127

Jessie had seen enough wounds to know that chewer had rended the young man's stomach and perhaps even other vital organs. Rafe was dying. The amazing part was that he was still alive and Jessie could only be thankful that every breath he took gave Ki and her Texans another moment to close the distance and rescue her.

"We'll wait an hour," Jeb snarled, taking up his buffalo rifle and mounting his horse.

"Where you goin'!" Henry demanded, alarm high in his voice.

"I'm going to find me an ambush place and kill the sonofabitch carrying a bow and an arrow!"

Jessie's mouth went dry with fear. She had little doubt that Jeb, with that big rifle of his, was a marksman. She wanted to jump up and somehow warn Ki but she was helpless.

Jessie closed her eyes and said a little prayer for Ki. And that Rafe would keep breathing long enough for her friends to come to her aid.

Two miles back, Ki reined in his horse and dismounted. He bent beside the tracks that they were following and studied them very carefully.

"This one horse is carrying double," he told Len. "You can see how much deeper the hoofprints are. And look at this."

Len also dismounted and knelt to stare at the dark spot that Ki brought to his attention. "Blood?"

"Exactly," Ki said. "And I've seen plenty more."

"Then you must have hit him with an arrow."

"Yes," Ki said, climbing back onto his horse. "They're close now. Let's hurry."

Ki and Len pushed their already heavily lathered horses back into a gallop. The sun was glaring down at them with surprising intensity given that it was still morning.

Ki was so busy staring down at the tracks that he did not see Jeb raise his powerful buffalo rifle and take careful aim.

128

"Ki!" Len shouted. "Look out!"

Ki acted instinctively. He threw himself off his running horse just as the buffalo rifle roared from a quarter mile away and belched a cloud of smoke. The samurai's horse took the heavy ball in the forehead and it dropped as if its legs had been chopped off at the knees. The horse somersaulted and lay twitching in death as Ki rolled and then flattened on the ground.

"He's shooting black powder!" Len cried. "I can kill him before he can reload!"

"No!" Ki shouted.

But his warning was in vain. Already, Len was tearing his Winchester carbine from his saddle boot and spurring his horse forward, intent on killing the big man in the buffalo robe.

Ki jumped to his feet and raced after the young man as he watched the buffalo hunter reload his black powder rifle with amazing speed.

Len unleashed three rounds at the man who stood so thick and unruffled. But when the big man finished reloading and threw his buffalo rifle to his shoulder, Len had enough sense to realize his peril. He reined sharply to one side, dropped Indian-style to the off side of his horse and when the big rifle boomed again, felt his mount crumble.

Len tried to throw himself away from his dying horse but he didn't quite succeed. The animal slammed down to the earth and Len felt his leg burn like fire and then go numb under the horse's weight. When they came to a stop, the horse began to thrash and try to regain its feet, but it was dying.

As he ran, Ki reached over the back of his shoulder and grabbed an arrow. He nocked it on the run and ran right on by his young friend. As the buffalo hunter again finished loading, Ki skidded to a halt, drew back his arrow, and fired.

The arrow arched high because the distance was more than a hundred yards. But its flight ran true and Ki saw the big man with the big rifle stagger and bat at his shoulder, then heard him curse as his rifle exploded harmlessly into the air.

The man dropped his buffalo rifle, jumped on his horse, and galloped over a hill.

Ki twisted to see Len struggling desperately to pull his leg out from under his horse. The samurai hated to break off his pursuit but he could not leave Len in such dire straits.

"Here," he said, running over to the young cowboy, dropping his bow, and grabbing his horse's foreleg. "When I pull, use your free leg to push against the saddle."

Len gritted his teeth against the pain and nodded to indicate that he understood.

"Now!"

Ki pulled with all his strength and Len, his neck corded with tendon, pushed with his free leg and managed to get the leg free.

The samurai dropped by his friend's side. "I've got to go after them. Can you walk?"

"No," Len said miserably.

Ki pulled up the cowboy's pants leg and stared at the leg which was already starting to turn purple and swell.

"Is it broken?"

"I don't think so," Ki said, "but it'll feel like it for a couple of days."

Len grabbed his forearm. "Go after Miss Starbuck. Don't worry about me. I got a canteen, some food in my saddlebags, and a gun."

"I'm going to take your rifle," Ki said. "I'm almost out of arrows."

Len managed a weak grin. "I always knew that, when it came down to it, you'd use a rifle."

Ki shook his head and stood up. "Only as a last resort," he said as he turned and began to run toward the low hill where the big man had disappeared.

Len twisted around and watched the samurai run. He did not think that Ki had a chance of saving Jessie on foot given that the men they followed were all mounted.

A moment later, however, Len took hope in remembering one very important fact—Ki had never failed Miss Jessica Starbuck before, and there was no reason to believe he would now.

★

Chapter 18

When Jessie had first heard the heavy thunder of the buffalo rifle, she'd wanted to jump up and run, but Henry had grabbed her by the throat, yanked his knife free and said, "Don't you even think about movin' your finger from my brother's gut."

Jessie swallowed and held her breath, then they'd heard the sound of a Winchester rifle being fired and then the huge buffalo rifle again. After that, there had been an ominous silence.

Henry relaxed and grinned with confidence. "Old Jeb, he never misses with that big buffalo rifle. Neither do I."

The man released her throat and Jessie gasped for air, then turned her face away so that Henry could not read her frightened thoughts.

"Here he comes!" Henry shouted, jumping up and striding out toward his brother.

132

Jessie never wanted more than anything in her life to jump up and run, but there was no place to run that they could not quickly overtake her from horseback. Besides, she'd been warned what would happen if she left Rafe's side.

The young man was very near death. Jessie had taken his pulse every few minutes and it was growing slower and weaker. His color was waxy, his breathing labored. Jessie was quite certain that young Rafe was bleeding to death internally. The man's death gave her no joy, but neither did she believe it would leave a void in this world.

Jeb threw himself off his horse, seemingly indifferent to the broken shaft of an arrow embedded in his massive shoulder.

Henry's eyes grew wide as he stared at the broken arrow and the spreading bloodstain. "He got you too!"

Jeb stomped over and snatched Rafe's buffalo rifle. His face was white and strained but his voice was as hard as ever.

"There's just two of them," he said to Henry. "The one with the bow and arrows and another one. Looked like a cowboy."

"Did you get them both?"

"No," Jeb swore. "I shot their horses though. One was pinned under his horse, the other, he didn't look like he wanted any . . ."

"Jeb, look!"

They all turned to see Ki running swiftly toward them with a Winchester clenched in his hands.

"The sonofabitch must be crazy!" Henry shouted. "Him with that carbine against us with buffalo rifles."

"I'm just glad he ain't shooting that bow," Jeb hissed as he frantically began to load Rafe's rifle. "Damn you, Henry, don't watch the bastard, shoot him!"

Henry dropped to the earth and took careful aim. A second later, his rifle belched a great cloud of smoke but when Jessie could see through it, she saw Ki jumping up from the ground and coming on.

"Sonofabitch!" Henry cursed.

Jeb sat down and laid Rafe's rifle atop his left knee and took aim. Just as he was squeezing the trigger, Jessie saw the samurai throw himself sideways. The rifle boomed but there was no doubt that Jeb had missed again. The huge man stared in astonishment and when he began to reload, Jessie saw him spill black powder because his hands were beginning to shake.

Ki fired two more rounds at them. His bullets sounded puny compared to the buffalo rifles, but Jessie saw that one slug kicked up dirt in Henry's face and caused him to panic.

"What . . ."

"Load!" Jeb bellowed, working over his rifle with sweat running into his eyes.

Jessie glanced at the horses and knew what she had to do. She jumped up and waving her arms, she yelled, "Yaaaa! Yaaa, horses! Git!"

"I'll kill her!" Jeb shouted, coming to his feet.

Jessie paid the man no attention. She tried to grab one of the horses and mount but they stampeded out of reach so she just kept running away, hoping and praying that Jeb or Henry didn't blow a hole in her spine with their huge rifles.

Ki saw Jessie run and when the larger of the two buffalo hunters jumped up to go after her and the horses, Ki unleased two quick bullets, having no time to aim. He got lucky though, because one of them struck Jeb in the behind and the man howled and dropped his rifle. Ki stopped, took aim, and drilled the big man through the chest.

"Run, Jessie!"

Henry saw his big brother clutching his buttocks and then suddenly slap at his chest. He saw Jeb's mouth form a silent scream as he stared into the hot, blazing sun. And then, Henry saw Jeb crash to the earth.

Henry's nerve broke. He dropped his rifle and ran after Jessie and the horses. He was tall and he was swift.

134

Gaining rapidly on Jessie, he overhauled her and again reached for his bowie knife.

"Woman!" he screamed, "I'm gonna gut you!"

Jessie could almost feel the man's breath on the back of her neck. She knew that she could not outrun him and that he fully intended to bury his blade in her before racing on to catch himself a horse.

Jessie stopped, spun around, and planted her feet. Henry, not expecting this and almost overtaking her, tried to stop but momentum carried him forward and Jessie threw herself at the man's knees.

Henry flew over her, his arms windmilling, and when he landed his own bowie knife was driven to the hilt in his side. Henry screamed, rolled over, and tried to get up. The horses were getting away!

"Jessie, get down!"

Jessie dropped and the samurai fired twice, both bullets tearing through Henry's thick buffalo coat and jerking his body first one way and then the other.

Ki dropped the Winchester and waited as Jessie came to her feet, then ran into his arms.

"Oh," she cried, hugging the samurai with all her might, "you were wonderful!"

Ki's chest swelled with pride. "And a little lucky," he admitted, removing his shirt and giving it to Jessie. "I'm not that good of a shot."

Jessie buttoned the shirt up to her neck but it still didn't cover her bottom. "I didn't even know you could use a rifle."

He nodded, unwilling to release her. "A samurai uses the traditional weapons of his ancestors. But a wise samurai prepares himself to also use modern weapons."

Jessie laughed. She pulled out of his arms and kissed his cheeks, one, then the other.

"You will always surprise me," she said. "And you will always be my hero."

Ki bowed very formally. A mask dropped over his face as he remembered that the old *ronin*, Hirata, had told him that a samurai must never allow his heart to betray his detached logic.

"I am your servant," he said. "And if I am also your hero and friend, then I am very fortunate indeed."

Jessie sighed. Ki might surprise her in many ways, but he would always remain, first and foremost, samurai.

"Len is down back over that hill," Ki said. "I expect he's going crazy wondering if we're going to appear or if the buffalo hunters are going to ride over and finish him off."

"Then I guess we'd better give him some peace of mind," Jessie said, "just as soon as I can find some more clothes to wear. Is Len hurt badly?"

"No. His leg is going to be pretty swollen and painful for a week or so, but other than that, he'll be fine. But I'm afraid that Bob Hanes is dead."

Jessie swallowed and then listened as Ki told her about how the cowboy had taken a heavy caliber ball in the chest last night.

Jessie shook her head and bit her lower lip before she managed to say, "We'll bury him this morning. I guess I was foolish to allow myself to hope that no one would get killed on this trail drive."

"It wasn't your fault," Ki said.

"I know." Jessie said, wondering if she would be forced to wear one of the dead buffalo hunter's pants until she could return to the Circle Star camp and reclaim her own clothing.

As if he could read her thoughts, Ki said, "You could wear one of those long buffalo robes back to our camp."

"How about if *you* wore one of them and I wore your pants?" Jessie asked.

Ki did not like the idea at all but since it was his purpose in life to serve Jessie, he nodded and began to remove the rest of his clothing.

★

Chapter 19

Sonny Lane handed his reins to Otis Rudd and moved to a little higher ground for a better view. It was early morning and he could see the Circle Star herd grazing along the banks of the Canadian River. He did not move for almost an hour despite the heat and the persistent flies.

When Sonny finally did come to his feet, he moved back down to Otis and his men with a wide smile on his handsome face.

"We're in big luck," he said, jerking his thumb over his shoulder back toward the herd. "The gawddamn samurai and some of the other cowboys are gone."

"Where?" Otis asked in a raspy voice forever altered by the blade of a Mexican's knife.

"I don't know," Sonny said. "But who the hell cares! The fact is, we'll never have a better opportunity to steal that herd than right now. They were shorthanded when

I rode out, they're even worse now."

Otis scrubbed his narrow jaw. He was a tall man, like Sonny Lane, but that was the only physical characteristic that they shared in common. Otis was horse-faced and his nose was broken. His eyes were spaced closely together and one of them wouldn't close properly, thanks to the same Mexican whose bones Otis had made sure were rotting in the Sonoran Desert.

"How many?"

"I counted just eight. The women are probably sleeping under the chuckwagon. Remember, I want Jessica Starbuck. You can have the little halfbreed girl."

Otis twisted around in his saddle. He studied his men and they were a hard, ugly collection of misfits. Four of them were Mexicans, four more were at least half Indian, and those that were whites were mostly fugitives from the law. They added up to an even dozen including himself and Sonny Lane.

Otis didn't count much on Sonny. He thought the man was more show than fight. Anybody as pretty in the face as Sonny wasn't to be trusted.

"Well?" Sonny prodded anxiously. "We gonna do it, or just sit here and watch the damned sun come up to burn our asses off?"

"Relax," Otis told him as he pulled his gun and spun the cylinder. He liked to ride with five bullets in the chamber but when he was ready to go into action, he wanted that sixth slug for insurance.

The misfits watched, knowing that this meant that they would soon be doing some killin' and cattle rustling. And if there were some women, like Sonny promised, they'd do some pleasurin', after Otis, of course.

The misfits grinned as they checked their own weapons. Two of the Mexicans also examined their carbines. The whole thing didn't take more than a few minutes but during it all, Sonny couldn't keep still.

"I'm telling you," he said, his voice edgy. "If we ride over this hill and strike right now, we'll catch them by surprise. But they'll be waking up any damn minute. I

138

don't understand what the hell you are waiting for, Otis!"

Otis swung his quirt and it made a harsh, whistling sound as it cut the air and slashed Sonny's handsome face. Sonny yelped, started to reach for his gun, but three of Otis's men were already pointing their pistols at his heart.

Sonny froze. Two long welts marred his cheeks and one of them oozed a little blood.

Otis grinned. Tapped the quirt against his leg. "Anything else you want to say?" he asked quietly.

Sonny tried but failed to swallow because he had no spit. He shook his head and touched his cheeks. When he saw blood on his fingers, he shook with a mixture of fear and fury.

Otis turned away from the man in disgust. His riders might be ugly misfits, but they knew when to fight, when to fuck, and when to keep their mouths shut.

"Santos, Escobar, Chili, and Ray. You men come in from the north. Smoky, you, Bill, and Charlie come in from the south. Me, Sonny, Isaac, and Mace will hit them from the east."

The men knew that Otis was taking the best line because he would be attacking straight out of the rising sun. Even so, they bore Otis no hard feelings or envy because, when you were the leader, you made the calls.

"We'll go at them just as soon as you're ready," Otis ordered. "Five minutes at the outside."

"No survivors, right?" Chili asked with a wide grin.

"None except for the women," Otis told the grinning Mexican. "Them and the cattle."

The group split up and Otis rolled a cigarette with one hand without spilling a single shred of tobacco. Sonny hated the ugly bastard for lashing him in the face and for being so cool. Why, the cutthroat sonofabitch was as steady as a rock. He even looked happy!

"You gonna do what you have to do?" Otis asked, breaking the morning silence.

Sonny blinked, then jerked his chin up and down rapidly. "You bet I am!"

"Sure you don't have a few friends down in that camp?"

"No friends," Sonny said bitterly. "When Jessie gave me my back pay and told me to get out, not a man among them offered a kind or encouragin' word. Not for all the times we rode together or any damn thing."

"You're breaking my heart," Otis hissed in contempt. "What the hell do you care if they said anything nice about you or not? You a goddamn man, or a woman!"

Sonny's cheeks flamed even higher when Otis laughed. Sonny had to grip his saddlehorn to keep his hand from jumping to the butt of his gun.

"When I got Jessie in my grasp," he stuttered in anger, "you'll see what a man can do to a wildcat woman. You just wait."

"Sure," Otis told him, lighting his cigarette, taking a long pull, and then letting the smoke trail out his nostrils. "I bet we'll all just be impressed as hell the way you poke the pork to her."

Sonny blushed with humiliation and longed to smash Otis's face into a bloody pulp. He could do it, too, in an even-up fist fight. And he knew that it wasn't *what* Otis said that cut a man to his core, it was *how* he said it. Mocking. Contemptuous. Disdainful. All of these words failed to describe how the ugly outlaw could render a man impotent and make him feel foolish.

Otis smoked with obvious relish. He smoked his damned cigarette right down to his fingers so that his own flesh burned and stunk and then he ground the cigarette butt out on his saddlehorn.

"Let's go have some fun," he said with a devilish grin.

Sonny managed to nod his head, hating how the other men looked at their leader with such respect. The sonofabitch isn't human, Sonny told himself. He's got ice water or whiskey instead of blood.

"Let's go!" Otis hissed, drawing his gun again and spurring over the hill.

Sonny saw a cowboy, he thought it was Moses Dial, step out from the bushes by the river as he buttoned his fly. Otis's gun bucked and Moses grabbed his crotch and did an absurd little dance before he pitched over and lay still.

A moment later, the entire camp was being overrun by Otis's men. Scotty Duggan fought from his chuckwagon. He killed one of the halfbreeds and wounded another before a bullet finally dropped him. Hank Potter emptied his gun, emptied a saddle, and then took a shot in the leg. Somehow he managed to save his life by jumping into the Canadian River and swimming as long and as hard as he could underwater.

Pete Willis had been riding the last watch and when he saw the raiders fly in at the herd, he drew his gun and rode straight at them. He killed two men before he was riddled with bullets and his horse thundered off with empty stirrups flapping.

When Sonny reached the camp, he dismounted on the run. He tore open the back of the chuckwagon and saw Donita with a big pistol clenched in her little fists.

She closed her eyes and fired at him point-blank but missed. Sonny tore the big Colt from her hands.

"Where's Jessie!"

"She's gone," Donita cried. "Let go, you're hurting me!"

Sonny twisted her arm even harder. "Where is she!"

"Some buffalo hunters took her away. Ki and some of the men went after them."

Sonny knew that she was telling the truth. It was the only explanation that made any sense. He poked his head out the back of the chuckwagon and saw that the fighting was almost over. There were dead Circle Star cowboys lying all over the place, but there were also a lot of riderless horses.

When the gunfire died, Otis yanked his horse up to a standstill beside the wagon. He took one look at Donita and said, "That one's mine."

"No!" Sonny's response had been automatic. He lowered his voice. "Miss Starbuck and the samurai are gone. I . . . I want this girl."

141

"Never!" Donita cried, spitting in his face.

Sonny backhanded her across the mouth and she crumpled like wet paper.

Otis laughed with contempt. "Some ladies' man you are!"

Sonny snapped. Donita's Colt had fallen between them and Sonny's hand wrapped itself around the butt. He brought the Colt up, knowing that Otis could not see it in the dim interior of the wagon.

"Funny is it?" Sonny asked, raising his eyebrows in question and ignoring the spittle on his face.

"You goddamn right it is!" Otis cackled.

Sonny didn't even raise the Colt but fired it from down by his waist. One moment Otis's mocking grin was there, the next moment there was nothing left but a bloody smear where the man's jaw had been quivering.

Donita screamed. Sonny watched Otis topple from his horse.

"Stop it!" Sonny yelled dropping the Colt as if it was molten metal. "Goddamn you, stop screaming and let me think or we're both dead!"

Donita stopped.

"All right," Sonny whispered frantically. "I didn't kill him. You did!"

"What!"

"That's right." Sonny's mind was racing now. Trying to come up with some way to save his own life, maybe Donita's as well.

"He . . . he grabbed for you and you shot him."

"But they'll torture me to death for that!"

"No! There's no time," Sonny said with a rush. "We've got to get the cattle out of here before the others come back. You tell them that there are many more men coming back."

"But . . ."

Sonny grabbed her by the shoulders and shook Donita so hard her head whipped back and forth on her shoulders. "It's our only chance. I can take command. We can get out of this alive and maybe rich if we stick together."

142

"I would rather die than have you or them touch me!" she hissed.

Sonny wanted to kill the crazy bitch. But instead, he forced himself to speak slowly. "I won't touch you, then. I swear it. And . . . and if there are any wounded out there, I'll see if I can save their lives. But you got to do as I say or we're both finished."

Donita looked into his eyes. She hated this man but she could not help but believe him.

"Will you do it?" he pleaded. "For us and for whoever else out there might be alive."

Donita nodded.

Sonny expelled a deep breath. "All right then, you let me do all the talking and we might just live through the next few minutes."

"All right," she heard herself say.

Sonny almost kissed her with gratitude, but she pulled away, her face contorted with hatred and loathing.

"Okay, okay," he breathed, backing out of the chuckwagon and pulling her after him. "So I do all the talking and the game right now is to keep breathing."

Donita tumbled out of the wagon. She saw the dead Circle Star cowboys and she began to sob. Let Sonny do the talking, she thought, I couldn't talk even if I wanted to.

The outlaws had paid a heavier price than they'd expected. Besides Sonny, there were just eight men left in any condition to ride. One of their numbers lay wheezing away his last breaths with a bullet in his lungs. Three more were shot stone dead.

Sonny did not elaborate his account when he spoke to the outlaws. In a very few words, he told them that Donita had shot Otis to death, and now she was going to be his woman. As for the herd, they would drive it on to Kansas, and there would be a bigger share for everyone now that their numbers had been considerably reduced.

The outlaws showed a complete lack of sorrow for either Otis or their fallen compadres.

143

"I know this herd and I can show you how to drive it to a market," Sonny told them. "You need me and I need this woman."

No one argued the point. The one named Charlie said, "If there's more coming, we'd better take all their horses and maybe still lay a trap for them."

"Yeah," Sonny said. "Sure. Good idea. So let's move!"

The outlaws reined their horses around and spurred into the herd. In less than five minutes, they had the entire Circle Star remuda as well as the herd moving northeast toward Kansas.

Sonny, with the beautiful halfbreed girl riding alongside, could not believe his great good fortune. Sure, Jessie and the samurai and a few cowboys would come after them. But the odds were still more than favorable, and just being alive seemed a miracle.

"You stick with me," he said, feeling a rush of confidence. "I'm going to get these cattle to market and when I do, I'll buy you the fanciest dress and shoes in Kansas."

In answer, Donita spat at the dirt. Sonny took a hard swing at her but the halfbreed girl was expecting it and ducked.

"I'm going to teach you how to respect a man," he swore.

"How you gonna do that," she challenged, "when there are none around?"

The hell with her, Sonny thought. If he made it to Kansas, he'd be able to have all the women he wanted, and this halfbreed bitch could earn a dress and a fancy pair of shoes working on her back.

★

Chapter 20

"Oh my God!" Jessie cried, spurring the buffalo hunter's horse down toward the wreckage of her camp. "No!"

Ki raced after her leaving Len to come up behind, face bloodless with the pain that radiated out from his injured leg.

"Miss Jessie?" a voice called from the trees down by the river.

She whirled, hand dropping to the gun on her hip where it froze. "Hank!"

Hank Potter, a gun in his own fist, wobbled out of the trees. His clothes were soaking wet and he was covered with mud. Jessie saw that he'd wrapped a strip of cloth around his wounded leg.

"The rustlers hit just a little after first light," Hank whispered. "Came in from three directions and gunned us down before we could really get set and put up a good fight. There are a couple more of us hiding down there by the water, but they're too shot up to move."

Tears streamed down Jessie's cheeks as she and Ki hurried down to the banks of the Canadian. Mike Mays and Art Volk were both wounded, but Jessie could see they would survive.

With Ki's help, she got all the wounded men up to the chuckwagon. For almost an hour she worked intently removing several bullets, then cleaning and bandaging wounds.

"We'll see that the men that did this pay," Jessie vowed.

"Get the herd back," Art said through clenched teeth. "You get them back and we'll be ready to push them the rest of the way to Abilene."

"We'll see," Jessie said.

Mike said, "Did you hear that Sonny Lane was leadin' them?"

Jessie blinked with surprise and then looked to Ki who arched his eyebrows indicating that he had not heard this piece of news either.

"No," Jessie said, "and I'm sorry to hear it."

"The traitor took Donita with him," Art said. "I wanted to try and stop him, but they'd have gunned me down."

"You did the right thing," Jessie said. "We'll bury our dead and go after all of them. They can't be that hard to overtake."

"I'm going with you," Len said. "I mean to help."

"With that leg?"

"It'll trouble me a mite," Len admitted, "but it won't stop me."

"All right," Jessie said, knowing that she and Ki were desperate for help.

Ki was the only man among them that was fit enough to dig graves so Jessie worked right alongside him.

"I wish now that we'd never started this ill-fated trail drive," she bitterly complained.

"It wasn't your fault," Ki said, digging furiously in the soft, riverside earth. "You and Ed Wright did what

146

had to be done in order to save the cattle. You had no choice."

Jessie knew he was right, but that didn't make her feel any better.

It was late afternoon when they finished burying the Circle Star cowboys. In the shade of the huge cottonwood trees, Jessie stood with tears flooding down her cheeks and with bowed head as she struggled to say a few parting words.

"Lord," she began, "you know that these were all good men. They were honest and loyal to the brand they rode for. They gave their lives without hesitation trying to save our herd. I will contact any and all family they have in this world, but I would appreciate it if You would welcome them into Your heavenly kingdom. Amen."

Jessie replaced her hat on her head. She went to her palomino who stood waiting.

"Let's go," she said, jamming her boot into her stirrup and mounting.

The three wounded men she was leaving behind stood looking forlorn and defeated.

Jessie could not ride away without saying, "You men are probably thinking that maybe you should or could have done something different and saved some of those we just buried. Well, I'm thinking the same thoughts myself but they're destructive and will serve us no good purpose."

"I just wish to God we could *do* something!" Art choked.

"You can," Jessie said. "You can mend your bodies and be ready to ride just as soon as we drive those cattle back. I'll need each of you. Getting our herd to market is what our friends died for and that's what we're going to do."

Her men nodded grimly. "Kill 'em, every last damn one," Hank Potter grated.

"How many left with my herd?" Jessie asked.

"Eight, maybe nine. There wasn't much time to count. You can't give them any chance, Miss Starbuck. They didn't give us one. Just ambush 'em and show no mercy."

Jessie, Ki, and Len exchanged glances and an unspoken pledge passed between them. They would have no choice but to kill the outlaws in order to recapture the herd.

"Let's ride," Jessie said, wondering if Len could possibly ride the way they were going to ride in order to overtake the herd. The man's leg would be killing him, but Len was the kind of cowboy that would pass out before he'd complain.

They crossed the Canadian River and followed the wide swath of hoofprints northeast toward Kansas. All afternoon and until dusk they galloped with Len holding on until midnight, when he toppled silently from his horse.

"We'll rest a few hours," Jessie said. "The horses need a rest."

Jessie untied her saddlebags and sat down beside her poor cowboy. "That leg must be giving you fits, huh?"

"It's a worry," Len admitted. "But all I need is just a little rest and it'll be fine."

"Are you sure?"

He nodded vigorously. "You need me, Miss Starbuck. Even with Ki, you still need me."

"You're right," Jessie conceded. "But I won't take you into a fight that you are too weak to have a chance of surviving. I've lost too many good men already."

"I'll hold my own," Len vowed. "Just get them in my rifle sights and I'll help you settle the score."

"Let's all get some rest," Jessie said, stretching out, using her saddle as a pillow. "We'll need to be clearheaded tomorrow when we overtake them."

They awoke a few hours before dawn and the air was warm but humid. The stars were fading quickly and when Jessie looked out toward their horses, she saw that Ki's mount was gone.

The samurai had slipped away in the night and Jessie knew that he had felt compelled to go on ahead and overtake the herd and the cattle rustlers. She just prayed that he wouldn't do anything without their help.

"Wake up," Jessie said to Len. "Ki has gone ahead and we need to catch up with him as quickly as we can."

Len awoke with a start.

"Here," Jessie said, handing the cowboy her canteen and a silver flask.

"What's this?"

"Whiskey. It will cut the pain a little."

"Uh-uh," he grunted. "It might make this leg feel better but it would throw my shooting off. There won't be any time for misses when we overtake those men."

Jessie smiled. She appreciated Len's sacrifice. "At least have some water and a couple of biscuits that Scotty Duggan . . ."

Jessie's throat tightened with the memory of her cranky but brave and dear camp cook.

"No thanks," Len said, shaking his head. "Scotty was a hell of a fine old man, but he couldn't cook worth a damn. Everyone knew that."

"Yeah," Jessie admitted. "But I guess he was so well-liked and respected that none of us had the heart to say how bad his cooking was."

They sat crosslegged on the prairie watching the eastern horizon start to glow with the first rays of sunrise.

"We'd better get saddled and ride," Jessie said as the sun poked its way over the hills.

Len nodded and used his Winchester to help lever himself to his feet. "That's going to be a pretty sunrise," he observed. "I just hope that you, me, and Ki get to see it go down this evening."

"Me too," Jessie said. "Me too."

Despite his protestations, Jessie had to give Len a boost so that he could mount. But once he managed to get his feet back in the stirrups, he worked up a brave smile and said, "I got something I want to talk to you about this morning."

149

Jessie mounted and they both put their horses into an easy lope. Jessie glanced sideways at the tall, buck-toothed cowboy with his freckles and boyish grin. In his own way, Len was a damn good-looking man.

"Go ahead and talk," Jessie said. "Until we either sight the herd or Ki, there's not a hell of a lot else we can do."

"It's about that halfbreed girl."

Jessie frowned. "What about her?"

"I love her," Len blurted out.

Not knowing how to react, Jessie just kept her green eyes straight ahead.

"Did you hear what I just said, Miss Starbuck?"

"I heard."

"And?"

"And why are you telling me this?"

"Well, you said to stay away from her. I wanted you to know that I've obeyed that order to the letter."

"Good."

"But I also wanted you to know that I'm going to ask her to marry me when we reach Abilene."

Now Jessie turned to look at him. "What?"

"I'm going to ask her to marry me," Len said with conviction. "Because if I don't, someone sure as hell will. And I'll never find a prettier or braver girl than Miss Donita."

"I can't argue with you on that score," Jessie said. "But I'd hoped that she would return to the Circle Star Ranch and live with us a while. She's confused and she's been badly hurt, Len. I think she needs some time to sort things out."

"Maybe," he said. "But if she does, then she'll tell me so. I can and I would wait."

Jessie rode on for several more miles. She liked Len very much and she had thought all along that, of all her cowboys, he was the one best suited for Donita.

"Maybe," Jessie said, "if you just got engaged, we could work out something where you could start taking cows instead of wages. After a year or two, I'd help you and Donita get a start on your own place if things were going in that direction."

"You'd do that much for me?"

"Sure. You're ready to give your life for my herd, aren't you?"

"Yes, but so are all the cowboys."

"That's right," Jessie said, "and I'd do the same for any one of them. Texas is a big country. There's room for ambitious men and strong women to start new ranches and raise families."

Len was about to say something but Jessie raised her hand and pointed. "There! Do you see the dust or my herd? We're only a few miles behind them now."

Whatever Len had been about to say was instantly forgotten. Talk of marriage and the future seemed silly considering that there was a very good chance that they would not live to have a future.

★

Chapter 21

Ki had overtaken the herd just after sunrise and once he'd established its true direction, the samurai had ridden hard to circle around it to the east.

Now, he saw that it was well that he had flanked the big herd of longhorns instead of coming directly up from behind because Sonny Lane was dropping three men behind to ambush any pursuers. Ki watched as the three rode their horses into a deep arroyo and dismounted. They tied their horses and yanked their Winchester rifles out of their saddle scabbards.

The samurai watched as Sonny galloped back to drive the herd on. Ki studied the lay of the land very carefully. He deeply regretted that it was broad daylight so that he could not make a fast approach on the three ambushers, but he was plenty willing to accept the challenge that he now faced.

Ki decided that he would have to abandon his horse and stalk his quarry on foot. He tied his horse in some brush beyond a low hill and left his rifle in favor of his bow, despite the fact that he only had two arrows remaining in his quiver. Ki then began to move stealthily from one piece of cover to another, coming in from behind the three outlaws.

It was easy, really. Had the three men been antelope, they would have looked for danger from each direction, but these men were expecting danger only from the south and never even glanced around behind them. When the samurai was less than twenty-five yards from the three men, he nocked his arrow and drew back the bowstring. The arrowhead he was forced to use was called a "cleaver" and it was crescent-shaped and specifically designed to sever ropes or bonds. Ki rarely used a "cleaver," but there was no choice this time so he took aim on the nearest man and let the arrow fly.

The outlaw took the arrow in the back and it severed his spine as Ki had supposed it would. Without a sound, the man tottered and then began to fall over backward. Before he struck the hard, dry earth, the samurai was unleashing his final arrow. It caught the second man in the side of the neck.

The outlaw screamed and batted frantically at his throat. The third man turned, stared in horror at his two companions and froze for an instant as Ki dropped his bow and snatched a *shuriken* star blade from his clothing.

Too late the man recovered from his shock and attempted to raise the barrel of his Winchester. Ki's arm and wrist snapped forward and the polished silver blade whirled silently to strike the outlaw in the forehead.

"Ahhh!" he screamed as blood cascaded down into his eyes before he pitched onto his face, driving the blade even deeper into his skull.

Ki turned back to look at the vanishing Circle Star herd. How many more, he wondered? Five or six? Maybe a few more. No matter. They would somehow kill them all and they'd save the halfbreed girl from whatever hell Sonny Lane had planned for her.

The samurai moved forward to the three dead men. One was a halfbreed, one a Mexican, and the other was just very ugly. They had probably all killed many times, as well as raped and plundered. They were the scum of the frontier and the samurai had no pity for them because they'd certainly not had any for Jessie's cowboys.

The samurai relieved the men of their holsters, pistols, and cartridge belts. He took the best sixgun and holster and strapped it around his waist and then selected the best rifle and horse. Overhead, a vulture had already either spotted or smelled fresh blood and began to circle. Very soon, he would be joined by others, and then Sonny Lane and the outlaws he commanded would know that death stalked them ever closer.

Ki started to mount one of the outlaw horses and ride on after the herd, but then he saw Jessie and Len galloping toward him.

The samurai stepped back down to earth. He suspected that Jessie would be highly annoyed that he had not waited for her and Len.

Ki was right. Jessie took one look at the grisly scene stretched out before her in the arroyo and shook her head. "I just wish you'd have awakened me and let me know your intentions. Ki, you can't do this alone."

"I am sorry," he said, meaning it. "I did not mean to anger you but you and Len were very tired. I thought that if I simply evened the odds just a little, it would be good."

"It is good," Jessie said, realizing she sounded irritable. "But you must promise me that you'll let us fight beside you from now on."

"I promise," Ki said sheepishly.

"Good."

Jessie looked away from the three dead men while Ki pulled his arrows out of them and then pried his *shuriken* star blade from the skull of the third.

"When do you think it would be best to attack the rest of them?" she asked.

"At sunset," Ki told her without hesitation. "We'll come at them right out of the sun. We'll rise up from some low spot in the ground and it will seem as if we are a swarm of hornets, only our stings will be bullets."

"If we do that, what's going to stop one of them from grabbing Donita and using her as a shield?" Len asked bluntly.

"Good question," Ki admitted. "My answer is that we kill them all before they can reach her."

Jessie bit her lower lip. "There's the entire herd to worry about too," she said. "If it weren't for Donita, I'd say that the best plan would be to stampede the herd right through their night camp."

"But there is the girl," Len said.

"Yes," Jessie said. "But maybe Ki could steal into camp and bring her out before we stampeded the herd."

The samurai nodded. "I could do that."

"Are you sure?" Len asked.

In answer, Ki made a sweeping gesture toward the three dead men and he didn't have to say a word because the implication was very clear. If he could stalk and kill three ambushers in broad daylight before they could even fire a shot to warn the others, he sure as hell could sneak into a night camp and save the beautiful halfbreed girl.

Jessie looked up at the sun. "This is a good place to wait. Sonny might come back or send others to see what happened to these men."

"I hope so," Len said.

"So do I," Ki echoed. "But I don't think he will. He'll be shorthanded now and when these three do not show up tonight, he'll remember the buzzards he saw circling overhead and he'll know that we are coming."

"Then it'll just be that much more difficult to get Donita out of his camp alive," Len fussed.

"Nothing is easy," Ki told him with a shrug of his broad shoulders before he lay down, covered his face with one of the dead outlaw's hats, and went to sleep.

155

Len gingerly dismounted and stared at the samurai. "If he weren't on our side, he would scare me out of my wits."

"But he is on our side," Jessie said. "And if the truth be known, he'd probably prefer to go into the outlaw's camp tonight wearing his *ninja* costume and with nothing but his knife and his martial arts skills."

Protest formed in the young man's eyes. "I couldn't stand to . . ."

"I know," Jessie said, anticipating his words. "And neither could I. That's why we are sticking with him through this thing tonight."

Len nodded. "I guess that, if the samurai saves her again, she won't have eyes for anyone but him."

"Jealousy at a time like this?" Jessie said in a teasing voice.

Len blushed. "Yeah. Pretty stupid, huh?"

"I'm afraid so," Jessie said. "But it's understandable. Still, Donita will realize the pain and the sacrifice you went through to help save her. It won't be overlooked, I promise."

"I hope not," the young man said. "Because I really do love her."

Jessie lay back on the ground and watched a second buzzard join the first as they wheeled around the bright orb of the sun. And although her lips were dry and cracking, she smiled, wondering what that traitorous Sonny Lane was thinking about right about now.

★

Chapter 22

"They're dead," Sonny muttered without preamble as the outlaws made a cold camp that night. "All three of them are dead."

A man named Holter glared at Sonny. "The hell you say they're dead. Those were good men we left behind."

"But not good enough," Sonny replied. "You boys saw the buzzards circling."

"Maybe they killed that woman and her samurai."

"Nope."

"Well how the hell can you be so damn sure!" Holter demanded.

"Because," Sonny told them all, "I know what the damned samurai can do. Just using his hands and feet, he can kill quicker than any of us can draw our guns and pull the trigger."

"Aw horseshit!"

Sonny hadn't expected them to believe him. They

were not the kind of men who believed in much of anything except blood, money, and bullets. He glanced sideways at Donita. Even angry, dirty, and disheveled, she was a real looker. Why hadn't he stayed in Jessica Starbuck's good graces and kept his job? He could have won this girl's heart and lovely body. He could have maybe had a little of Jessica as well.

Now, he was a man on the run with a herd of cattle that he knew he'd never be able to sell because everyone in Kansas knew the Circle Star brand. Hell, who was he fooling? He'd messed up his chances and now the samurai was on his way to get his revenge.

The samurai. How could he explain to these filthy fools that the samurai could and would kill them all? How could he tell them that their only chance was simply to resaddle their horses, scatter, and run for their lives?

Sonny knew that he couldn't tell them. "Who's going to take the first watch on the herd tonight?"

"Not me," a Mexican hissed.

"Me neither," a halfbreed said with contempt. "Why don't you take first watch? We'll watch the girl."

They laughed as if it were a big joke, and Donita actually shifted a little closer to Sonny, so terrible did these men look and sound.

"Okay," Sonny told them. "I'll take first watch."

The men gaped and then fixed their hunter's eyes on Donita as if she were fresh meat to devour.

Sonny stood up and grabbed her by the wrist. "But I'll take this one along to keep me company."

"Hey! She looks tired!" one of the outlaws said with a lascivious grin. "Why don't you let her sleep a while."

"Because the moment I was gone, she'd have all of you tearing off your pants and piling on her," Sonny said, contemptuously.

The outlaws didn't like that, but when Sonny pushed Donita out toward their horses, they chose not to make an issue of it.

"Sleep light," Sonny warned. "Because, if the samurai comes tonight, you'll spend forever in hell."

Sonny left them moving backward because he did not trust a single one. When he and Donita reached their horses, he saddled her horse and then his own. He tightened both cinches and he took four canteens and slung them over the saddlehorns.

"Thirsty?" Donita asked.

Sonny nodded. He took an extra Winchester and when he mounted he whispered, "Let's ride out around the herd just like we was gonna do it for the next couple of hours."

Donita frowned, still not understanding. She rode side by side with him around the herd and when they were across from the outlaw camp, Sonny reined his horse to follow the North Star.

"Where are you going?"

"We're leaving right now," Sonny answered. "By the time they wake up—if they wake up—we'll be miles to the north."

"But . . ."

"I guess you weren't listening either," Sonny told her. "The samurai and some of the Circle Star men are coming. They've already killed the three men I left behind and they'll kill me as well if I stay with this pack of mangy dogs. We're leaving."

"To go where?"

"I don't know," Sonny told her. "We're just getting as far away from this herd as we can. Maybe, if they kill the others and get the herd back, they'll let me go."

Donita saw that he was really scared. And when she thought about Ki and what he had done in the Comanche canyon, she understood why. Sonny had been there that time and he knew how deadly the samurai could be. Sonny was, she decided, wicked but also smart.

"And if I chose not to run but instead to be saved by my friends?"

Sonny spurred his horse up and grabbed her by the throat. "I could kill you right now," he hissed. "I could snap your neck like a twig and leave you twitching in the dirt."

159

"Please," she choked, "no!"

He tore the reins from her hand. "Then don't give me any grief, woman. We're going to ride the hell out of these horses and we're not going to look back."

Donita swallowed painfully. She would say no more and hope that Ki and whoever else was with him killed this crazy man before he killed her.

Two hours later, Ki raised his hand in the moonlight and drew his horse to a halt. Without a word, he dismounted and stepped between Jessie and Len's horses.

In a low whisper, he said, "The herd is just ahead of us. I think I should go in first."

Jessie nodded in agreement. "We'll stampede the cattle through their camp and shoot down as many as we can. Your job is to save the girl, if at all possible."

Len swallowed noisily, then stuck out his hand. "Good luck," he whispered.

"Thanks."

When Ki vanished into the darkness, Jessie said, "Good luck to you as well."

"Miss Starbuck?"

"Yes?"

"Win or lose, I'm mighty proud to ride for your brand."

Jessie smiled and rode away. She circled to the east knowing that Len would loop around the herd to the west. It occurred to her that she should have given the brave young cowboy some kind of a signal so that he would know when to charge in and start firing.

But hell, she thought, he'll know. When that herd starts to running, the devil himself will know.

★
Chapter 23

When Ki reached the edge of the outlaw camp, he saw a man sitting upright with a rifle balanced across his knees. The man was trying to stay awake but not doing a very good job of it. His chin kept dipping and then bouncing off his chest.

Ki looked at the other sleeping figures, silhouetted in the pale moonlight. He was searching for one that would belong to Donita. After several minutes, he frowned. All of the sleeping figures appeared too large to be that of the halfbreed girl. That meant that they must be keeping her apart from the others. Maybe Sonny was sleeping with her somewhere away from the camp. It made sense because the ex-Circle Star cowboy would know that Ki was coming on a vengeance trail.

Ki began to move around the perimeter of the camp, searching for Sonny and Donita. He was just about to give up when the guard's head dropped especially hard against his chest and the man awakened to see the samurai poised between himself and the cattle.

For a moment, the outlaw stared and Ki froze, hoping that the man would go back to sleep. But he didn't.

"Hey!" he yelled, throwing his rifle up and firing all in one smooth motion.

Ki leapt sideways and the first bullet missed, but the outlaw was so skillful with a rifle that a second bullet ricocheted off the samurai's ribs, breaking bone and tearing away a huge piece of muscle.

The samurai grunted with pain and found that the movement of his right arm was impaired. As another bullet exploded, Ki hit the dirt, rolled, and used his left hand to haul out a sixgun from his waistband. He fired twice at the guard and nailed him both times.

The other outlaws, half-asleep and confused, jumped up from their bedrolls and would have riddled the samurai except that Jessie and Len were already stampeding the herd at them.

It was all the samurai could do to spring to his feet and race headlong into the night trying to get out of the path of the stampede. He didn't know where Donita might be but he did know that getting himself trampled to death would serve no good purpose.

Ki swore he saw the old one-eyed brindle bull breathing smoke and fire as it charged by. The samurai thought he heard a scream that ended with terrifying abruptness, and he heard several more shots.

The longhorns thundered past, sweeping down everything in their path. Ki felt the earth shake beneath his feet and he did not stop running until he reached his horse and remounted, holding his wounded side.

Jessie came right on the heels of the herd. Her sixgun was clenched in her fist and when she saw a muzzle flash, she fired twice and it was extinguished as if it were a candle. Twice more she saw outlaws firing into the face of the herd in a futile attempt to turn the cattle from their path of destruction. Jessie killed one more man but not before he downed two of her steers.

It looked like an undulating sea filled with snakes as the backs of the huge longhorns mowed down the outlaw camp and their horns clashed like wooden swords. Jessie shivered to think what a frightening sight it would be to the outlaws who were being pulverized by thousands of sharp hooves. They would be little more than bloody smears on the hard dirt come morning.

When there were no more targets and no more outlaws standing, Jessie joined up with Len and he told her that he'd also shot two men.

"Let's find Ki and the girl," Jessie said.

Ki wasn't hard to find and when they were reunited again Jessie looked around, then said, "Where's Donita?"

"I couldn't find her," Ki confessed. "I looked all around the camp and she was gone."

Len groaned.

"No," Ki said quickly, "I'm sure that she wasn't in that camp and is still alive. In fact, I didn't see Sonny and I would have recognized his silhouette in the moonlight. My guess is that he took Donita and made a run for it."

"Then I'll go after him," Len said.

"We'll *all* go after him," Jessie countered.

"But the herd."

"They won't run for very long. We can gather them up on our way back."

Jessie made it sound as if they did such a thing every day of their lives, but Ki knew that she was risking everything in order to save the girl.

Suddenly, Jessie cried out, "Ki, you've been hit!"

"Just a scratch," he said.

"I'll be the judge of that," she said, "get down and let me have a look."

Ki dismounted and when Jessie pulled his shirt back to see the ugly flesh wound, she shook her head. "This is one hell of a lot more serious than just a 'scratch'."

"It'll be fine."

"I want you to ride back to our camp," Jessie said, "and bring the wounded boys here to gather the cattle.

163

That's what they'll want to do."

It was Ki's turn to blink with surprise. "Jessie," he said hurriedly, "I should go after Sonny and . . ."

"No," she said. "You've done everything so far. Now, it's our turn."

"But . . ."

"Ki," Jessie said, putting her hands on the samurai's shoulders, "it's important that Len be the man that saves Donita this time."

"Oh," said Ki, at last understanding. "But what if . . ."

"We'll be all right. The men need you and so does the herd."

The samurai didn't like this one bit but Jessie was the boss and he understood why it was important that Len save the girl. He loved her. A man needed to feel important to the woman he loved and Ki knew that Len was man enough to handle Sonny, especially with Jessie's help.

"I'll get the chuckwagon here and we'll gather the herd," Ki said. "We should have everything ready by day after tomorrow."

Jessie bandaged his side. "We'll be back by then," she promised. "With the girl."

When Jessie and Len galloped away in the darkness, the samurai stood watching their trail of dust rise toward the yellow moon for a long, long time.

They'll be fine, he told himself. And they'll save the girl.

★

Chapter 24

Jessie and Len had switched horses with the outlaws once more. By choosing the best and freshest of their horses and taking along two extras so that they could relay, they rapidly closed the distance on Sonny and Donita.

"There they are!" Len shouted, urging his horse ahead in the moonlight.

Jessie didn't know how the young man was staying in the saddle with his badly injured leg. Maybe he was just running on guts and adrenalin, but now she saw him pull his gun.

"No! Let's give him a chance to surrender."

"But he won't do that!"

Jessie strongly suspected Len was right but with Donita's life at stake, giving Sonny an alternative seemed prudent.

They both saw Sonny glance over his shoulder and then spur his horse into an even harder run.

"Shall we change horses!" Len shouted.

"Another mile," Jessie said, feeling her horse still had some wind and strength left to expend in this brutal chase across the dry prairie.

Overhead, the moon sailed behind a dark cloud and Jessie could feel the air freshening. Not far to the north, she saw a jagged spear of lightning lance down to strike the earth. A moment later, the prairie rocked with a heavy roll of thunder.

My God, she thought, maybe it's even going to rain.

On and on they ran and although they could see Sonny whipping and spurring his horse like a wild man, they were gaining ground.

"Now!" Jessie called.

She kicked her boots from the saddle, drew her relay horse up close, and made the running change effortlessly. It was a trick that she had learned as a girl but had never used before.

Len had more trouble because of his bad leg and, if Jessie had not actually grabbed him as he made the switch, he might well have taken a horrible fall between their racing horses.

They turned their used horses free and the animals peeled off to stagger to a halt and then lower their heads and blow hard for air.

With semifresh horses between their legs, Jessie could almost see the distance between herself and their quarry shrink with each lunging stride of the horses.

Sonny glanced over his shoulder once more and when he saw that he was quickly being overtaken, he did the only thing that made any sense—he tore Donita from her saddle, hauled his faltering horse to a standstill and drew his gun.

"Hold it!" he shouted.

Jessie and Len reined in hard. Jessie drew her gun and aimed it at the man. "It's over," she said, "let Donita go."

Sonny laughed a little crazily. "You must think I'm insane."

"I don't know what I think about you," Jessie said. "But let the girl go."

"Drop your guns or I'll kill her." To emphasize his point, he placed the barrel of his sixgun against Donita's temple and pulled back the hammer.

Jessie took a deep breath but she did not drop her sixgun.

"Miss Starbuck," Len whispered nervously, "what are we going to do?"

"We kill him and his horse," she heard herself say, "because if we throw down our guns, he kills us and then he takes her away."

"No!" Sonny shouted. "That's wrong. You drop your guns and I'll give up the girl and ride away. Then it'll be over between us. Right!"

Jessie shook her head. "You found outlaws and brought them back to steal my herd and murder my cowboys. Cowboys you rode with and that considered you their friend."

"They considered me as nothing!" Sonny cursed. "When you fired me, not one of them said so much as a goodbye or good luck."

"That's because they saw that you were mean inside," Jessie said. "Now drop the gun and we'll take you on to Abilene and the law will decide what it should do to you."

"Oh, no!" Sonny cried, his voice heightening with hysteria. "I'm not going to prison and I damn sure ain't going to hang!"

Jessie could see that the man wasn't going to give it up. The gun was shaking in his big fist and she was afraid that he would pull the trigger by accident if not on purpose.

"Miss Starbuck," Len stammered, "he's serious. He's going to blow her brains out."

"I know that," Jessie whispered, "so let's aim for his head which is the only open shot we have and let's pray we don't miss."

167

"But . . ."

Jessie didn't hear what else Len had to say. She fired and, a split second later, Len fired too. Donita screamed and Jessie thought for certain that one or the other of them had killed her, but Sonny threw up his big arms and clawed at the sky, then crashed over the back of his horse.

The horse bolted and tried to run but it was so weary that Len quickly overtook it and pulled the girl from the saddle.

In the pale moonlight, Jessie watched as Donita threw herself into Len's open arms.

She dismounted and with great weariness, she trod over to stand beside the body of Sonny Lane. She knelt beside the dead man noting the single neat bullet hole that entered his skull just at his hairline. Jessie was sure that it was her bullet that had killed the man but she'd tell Donita and Len she'd missed.

"You had the looks, the brains, the guts, and the charm to do about whatever you wanted in life," she said to the body. "And you sure could fool a woman into thinking she might like to get to know you real well. What a shame you were, Sonny Lane."

Jessie sighed and came back to her feet. She watched Len and Donita dismount and the tall cowboy tried to stand, but lost his balance on his one good leg and toppled to the earth, pulling the beautiful halfbreed girl down with him.

Donita laughed and began to kiss the cowboy. Jessie climbed wearily back into the saddle and reined south. Let the pair do what they needed to do. She would see them married in Abilene and, in time, they would have tall Texas children and raise good Texas longhorn cattle.

Another jagged bolt of lightning shivered down through the dark heavens and suddenly, Jessie felt a big wet raindrop smack her in the face. Almost instantly, more followed and soon she was drenched in a great downpour.

She heard Len whoop and holler with glee and Jessie turned her face up to the sky and let it open and wash her face.

The rain felt wonderful. As a cattlewoman, she knew that it would mean that soon, very soon, the prairie would regenerate and be covered with grass and flowers. Her cattle, thin and weak, would graze on into Abilene, sleek and fat.

Tears of gratitude mingled with the rain and Jessie smiled.

Watch for

LONE STAR AND THE HORSE THIEVES

115th in the exciting LONE STAR series
from Jove

Coming in March!

My name is Alfred Addlington. Some may find it hard to believe I was born in New York City. I never knew my mother. Father is a lord; I suppose you would call him a belted earl. The family never cared for Mother. Marrying a commoner if you are of the nobility is far worse, it was felt, than murdering someone.

I was, of course, educated in England. As a child I'd been an avid reader, and always at the back of my mind was this "horrible obsession" to one day become a Wild West cowboy. I'd no need to run away—transportation was happily furnished. While I was in my seventeenth year my youthful peccadillos were such that I was put on a boat bound for America, made an allowance and told never to come back.

They've been hammering outside. I have been in this place now more than four months and would never have believed it could happen to me, but the bars on my window are truly there, and beyond the window they are building a gallows. So I'd better make haste if I'm to get this all down.

I do not lay my being here to a "broken home" or evil companions. I like to feel in some part it is only a matter of justice miscarried, though I suppose most any rogue faced with the rope is bound to consider himself badly used. But you shall judge for yourself.

Seventeen I was when put aboard that boat, and I had a wealth of experience before at nineteen this bad thing caught up with me.

So here I was again in America. In a number of ways it was a peculiar homecoming. First thing I did after clearing customs was get aboard a train that would take me into those great open spaces I'd so long been entranced with. It brought me to New Mexico and a town called Albuquerque, really an overgrown village from which I could see the Watermellon Mountains.

I found the land and the sky and the brilliant sunshine remarkably stimulating. Unlike in the British Midlands the air was clean and crisply invigorating. But no one would have me. At the third ranch I tried they said, "Too young. We got no time to break in a raw kid with roundup scarce two weeks away."

At that time I'd no idea of the many intricacies or the harsh realities of the cow business. You might say I had on a pair of rose-colored glasses. I gathered there might be quite a ruckus building up in Lincoln County, a sort of large-scale feud from all I could learn, so I bought myself a horse, a pistol and a J. B. Stetson hat and headed for the action.

In the interests of saving time and space I'll only touch on the highlights of these preliminaries, recording full details where events became of impelling importance.

Passing through Seven Oaks, I met Billy, a chap whose name was on everyone's tongue, though I could not think him worth half the talk. To me he seemed hard, mean spirited and stupid besides. He made fun of my horse, calling it a crowbait, declared no real gent would be found dead even near it. Turned out he knew of a first class mount he'd be glad to secure for me if I'd put one hundred dollars into his grubby hand. He was a swaggering sort I was glad to be rid of. Feeling that when in Rome one did as the Romans, I gave him the hundred dollars, not expecting ever to see him again, but hoping in these strange surroundings I would not be taken for a gullible "greenhorn."

A few days later another chap, who said his name was Jesse Evans, advised me to steer clear of Billy. "A bad lot," he told me. "A conniving double-crosser." When I mentioned giving Billy the hundred dollars on the understanding he would provide a top horse, he said with a snort and kind of pitying look, "You better bid that money good-bye right now."

But three days later, true to his word, Billy rode up to the place I was lodging with a fine horse in tow. During my schooling back in England I had learned quite a bit about horses, mostly hunters and hacks and jumpers and a few that ran in "flat" races for purses, and this mount Billy fetched looked as good as the best. "Here, get on him," Billy urged. "See what you think, and if he won't do I'll find you another."

"He'll do just fine," I said, taking the lead shank, "and here's ten dollars for your kindness."

With that lopsided grin he took the ten and rode off.

I rode the new horse over to the livery and dressed him in my saddle and bridle while the proprietor eyed me with open mouth. "Don't tell me that's yours," he finally managed, still looking as if he couldn't believe what he saw.

"He surely is. Yes, indeed. Gave a hundred dollars for him."

Just as I was about to mount up, a mustached man came bustling into the place. "Stop right there!" this one said across the glint of a pistol. "I want to know what you're doing with the Major's horse. Speak up or it'll be the worse for you."

"What Major?"

"Major Murphy. A big man around here."

"Never heard of him. I bought this horse for one hundred dollars."

"Bought it, eh? Got a bill of sale?"

"Well, no," I said. "Didn't think to ask for one."

I'd discovered by this time the man with the gun had a star on his vest. His expression was on the skeptical side. He wheeled on the liveryman. "You sell him that horse?"

"Not me! Came walkin' in here with it not ten minutes ago."

"I'm goin' to have to hold you, young feller," the man with the star said, pistol still aimed at my belt buckle. "A horse thief's the lowest scoundrel I know of."

A shadow darkened the doorway just then and Jesse Evans stepped in. "Hang on a bit, Marshal. I'll vouch for this button. If he told you he paid for this horse it's the truth. Paid it to Billy—I'll take my oath on it."

A rather curious change reshaped the marshal's features. "You sure of that, Evans?"

"Wouldn't say so if I wasn't."

The marshal looked considerably put out. "All right," he said to me, "looks like you're cleared. But I'm confiscatin' this yere horse; I'll see it gits back to the rightful owner. You're free to go, but don't let me find you round here come sundown." And he went off with the horse.

"Never mind," Evans said. "Just charge it up to experience. But was I you I'd take the marshal's advice and hunt me another habitation." And he grinned at me sadly "I mean pronto—right now."

Still rummaging my face, he said, scrubbing a fist across his own, "Tell you what I'll do," and led me away out of the livery-keeper's hearing. "I've got a reasonably good horse I'll let you have for fifty bucks. Even throw in a saddle—not so handsome as the one you had but durable and sturdy. You interested?"

178

Once stung, twice shy. "Let's see him," I said, and followed him out to a corral at the far edge of town. I looked the horse over for hidden defects but could find nothing wrong with it; certainly the animal should be worth fifty dollars. Firmly I said, "I'll be wanting a bill of sale."

"Of course," he chuckled. "Naturally." Fetching a little blue notebook out of a pocket, he asked politely, "What name do you go by?"

"My own," I said. "Alfred Addlington."

He wrote it down with a flourish. "All right, Alfie." He tore the page from his book and I put it in my wallet while Jesse saddled and bridled my new possession. I handed him the money, accepted the reins and stepped into the saddle.

He said, "I'll give you a piece of advice you can take or cock a snook at. Notice you're packin' a pistol. Never put a hand anyplace near it without you're aimin' to use it. Better still," he said, looking me over more sharply, "get yourself a shotgun, one with two barrels. Nobody'll laugh at that kind of authority."

"Well, thanks. Where do I purchase one?"

"Be a-plenty at Lincoln if that's where you're headed. Any gun shop'll have 'em."

I thanked him again and, having gotten precise directions, struck out for the county seat feeling I'd been lucky to run across such a good Samaritan. I was a pretty fair shot with handgun or rifle but had discovered after much practice I could be killed and buried before getting my pistol into speaking position. So Evans's advice about acquiring a shotgun seemed additional evidence of the good will he bore me.

It was shortly after noon the next day when I came up the dirt road into Lincoln. For all practical purposes it was a one-street town, perhaps half a mile long, flanked by business establishments, chief amongst them being the two-storey Murphy-Dolan store building. I recall wondering if this was the Major whose stolen horse Billy'd

179

sold me, later discovering it was indeed. Leaving my horse at a hitch rack I went inside to make inquiries about finding a job.

The gentleman I talked with had an Irish face underneath a gray derby. After listening politely he informed me he was Jimmie Dolan—the Dolan of the establishment, and could offer me work as a sort of handyman if such wasn't beneath my dignity. If I showed aptitude, he said, there'd be a better job later and he would start me off at fifty cents a day.

I told him I'd take it.

"If you've a horse there's a carriage shed back of the store where you can leave him and we'll sell you oats at a discount," he added.

"I'd been hoping to get on with some ranch," I said.

"A fool's job," said Dolan with a grimace. "Long hours, hard work, poor pay and no future," he assured me. "You string your bets with us and you'll get to be somebody while them yahoos on ranches are still punchin' cows."

I went out to feed, water and put up my new horse. There was a man outside giving it some pretty hard looks. "This your nag?" he asked as I came up.

"It most certainly is."

"Where'd you get it?"

"Bought it in Seven Oaks a couple of days ago. Why?"

He eyed me some more. "Let's see your bill of sale, bub," and brushed back his coat to display a sheriff's badge pinned to his shirt.

I dug out the paper I had got from Evans. The sheriff studied it and then, much more searching, studied me. "Expect you must be new around here if you'd take Evans's word for anything. I'm taking it for granted you bought the horse in good faith, but I'm going to have to relieve you of it. This animal's the property of a man named Tunstall, stolen from him along with several others about a week ago."

I was pretty riled up. "This," I said angrily, "is the second stolen mount I've been relieved of in the past ten days. Don't you have any honest men in your bailiwick?"

"A few, son. Not many I'll grant you. You're talkin' to one now as it happens."

"Then where can I come by a horse that's not stolen?"

That blue stare rummaged my face again. "You a limey?"

"If you mean do I hail from England, yes. I came here hoping to get to be a cowboy but nobody'll have me."

He nodded. "It's a hard life, son, an' considerably underpaid. Takes time to learn, but you seem young enough to have plenty of that. How much did you give for two stolen horses?"

"One hundred and fifty dollars."

He considered me again. "You're pretty green, I guess. Most horses in these parts sell for forty dollars."

"A regular Johnny Raw," I said bitterly.

"Well . . . a mite gullible," the sheriff admitted. "Reckon time will cure that if you live long enough. Being caught with a stolen horse hereabouts is a hangin' offense. Come along," he said. "I'll get you a horse there's no question about, along with a bona fide set of papers to prove it. Do you have forty dollars?"

I told him I had and, counting out the required sum, handed it to him. He picked up the reins of Tunstall's horse, and we walked down the road to a public livery and feed corral. The sheriff told the man there what we wanted and the fellow fetched out a good-looking sorrel mare.

"This here's a mite better'n average, Sheriff—oughta fetch eighty. Trouble is these fool cowhands won't ride anythin' but geldin's. I guarantee this mare's a real goer. Try her out, boy. If you ain't satisfied, she's yours fer forty bucks."

The sheriff, meanwhile, had got my gear off Tunstall's horse. "Get me a lead shank," he said to the stableman. Transferring my saddle and bridle to the mare I swung onto her, did a few figure eights, put her into a lope,

181

walked her around and proclaimed myself satisfied. The animal's name it seemed was Singlefoot. "She'll go all day at that rockin' chair gate," the man said. "Comfortable as two six-shooters in the same belt."

Thanking them both, I rode her over to the nearest café, tied her securely to the hitch pole in front of it and went in to put some food under my belt, pleased to see she looked very well alongside the tail-switchers already tied there.

A special offer for people who enjoy reading the best Westerns published today.

WESTERNS!

NO OBLIGATION

Mail the coupon below

To start your subscription and receive 2 FREE WESTERNS, fill out the coupon below and mail it today. We'll send your first shipment which includes 2 FREE BOOKS as soon as we receive it.

Mail To: **True Value Home Subscription Services, Inc. P.O. Box 5235**
120 Brighton Road, Clifton, New Jersey 07015-5235

YES! I want to start reviewing the very best Westerns being published today. Send me my first shipment of 6 Westerns for me to preview FREE for 10 days. If I decide to keep them, I'll pay for just 4 of the books at the low subscriber price of $2.75 each; a total $11.00 (a $21.00 value). Then each month I'll receive the 6 newest and best Westerns to preview Free for 10 days. If I'm not satisfied I may return them within 10 days and owe nothing. Otherwise I'll be billed at the special low subscriber rate of $2.75 each; a total of $16.50 (at least a $21.00 value) and save $4.50 off the publishers price. There are never any shipping, handling or other hidden charges. I understand I am under no obligation to purchase any number of books and I can cancel my subscription at any time, no questions asked. In any case the 2 FREE books are mine to keep.

Name _____

Street Address _____ Apt. No. _____

City _____ State _____ Zip Code _____

Telephone _____

Signature _____
(if under 18 parent or guardian must sign)

Terms and prices subject to change. Orders subject
to acceptance by True Value Home Subscription
Services, Inc.

10790